Beth gulped for breath.

'All right, you asked for it,' she seethed. 'I think you're arrogant, ruthless and manipulative! And you're totally unscrupulous in the way you use your assets to convince people to do what you want. Just because you're loaded with power and money and sex appeal——'

'With what?' asked Daniel pleasantly.

'Sex appeal,' she stammered faintly.

'Yes, I thought that was what you said,' he murmured. 'But don't let me interrupt. Do continue...'

Dear Reader

This month finds us once again well and truly into winter—season of snow, celebration and new beginnings. And whatever the weather, you can rely on Mills & Boon to bring you sixteen magical new romances to help keep out the cold! We've found you a great selection of stories from all over the world—so let us take you in your mid-winter reading to a Winter Wonderland of love, excitement, and above all, romance!

The Editor

Angela Devine grew up in Tasmania surrounded by forests, mountains and wild seas, so she dislikes big cities. Before taking up writing, she worked as a teacher, librarian and university lecturer. As a young mother and Ph.D. student, she read romantic fiction for fun and later decided it would be even more fun to write it. She is married with four children, loves chocolate and Twinings teas and hates ironing. Her current hobbies are gardening, bushwalking, travelling and classical music.

Recent titles by the same author:

TAHITIAN WEDDING

THE BRIDE OF SANTA BARBARA

BY

ANGELA DEVINE

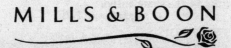

MILLS & BOON LIMITED
ETON HOUSE, 18-24 PARADISE ROAD
RICHMOND, SURREY TW9 1SR

To Marge Wheeler, Pat Roberts,
Sarah and Norman Sheegog,
with warm thanks for their help
and hospitality

*First published in Great Britain 1993
by Mills & Boon Limited*

© Angela Devine 1993

*Australian copyright 1993
Philippine copyright 1994
This edition 1994*

ISBN 0 263 78355 3
*Set in Times Roman 10 on 11½ pt.
01-9401-54857 C
Made and printed in Great Britain*

CHAPTER ONE

'OK, BETH. This is the most important day of your life. You're getting married today. So let's have a really big smile.'

With a hesitant tilt of her lips Beth turned to face the photographer. Behind him she could see the towering blue hills that rose like a painted backdrop behind the city of Santa Barbara. Above them the sun was just beginning to rise, sending a faint pink glow along the ridgetops and lighting up the palm trees and white stuccoed houses on the waterfront. The air was still moist and fresh with no hint of the heat that would blaze out later in the day. A gentle breeze blew from the land, sending a sound like wind chimes rippling through the masts of the yachts in the marina and ruffling her veil. She stole a swift glance behind her and saw that the ocean was taking on the same rosy pink hue of the sky. It was a perfect day for taking photos and a perfect day for a wedding. Feeling half shy and half foolish, Beth let her thoughts dwell on the prospect of marrying Warren. All the doubts of the last three years would be swept aside in one glorious moment. The uncertainties would be gone forever...

'You're frowning slightly, honey,' warned the photographer. 'I want a really big smile. Radiant. Joyful. Yes, like that.'

Finally Beth pushed away her doubts. A wistful look crept into her light blue eyes and a hesitant half-smile played around the corners of her wide mouth. She concentrated on happiness and suddenly her whole face lit up. Her lips parted into a beaming grin and the cleft in her chin grew more accentuated than ever.

'That's great!' exclaimed the photographer. 'Any time you want a job as a professional model, you just come straight to me. Now can you lean a little against the railings of the launch? Yes, like that. I want to catch the background of the harbour behind you.'

The varnished deck of the motor launch was bobbing gently under Beth's feet and the long white dress hampered her movements. But, looping her train cautiously over one arm, she did her best to obey his orders.

'See if you can actually sit up on the railing a little,' he urged. 'I want your curls fluttering in the breeze and the veil blowing out behind you. That's fine.'

Darting a swift glance over her shoulder, Beth saw the pearly pink curve of a sail gliding towards them across the water like the outstretched wings of a bird. She scrambled into a precarious position on the railing, pushed the lace veil out over her right shoulder and ran her long slim fingers through her blonde curls.

'Like this, Michael?' she asked.

'Great,' agreed the photographer. 'Now if you could just—— '

But what he was going to say Beth never found out, for at that moment there was a terrific thud and the cabin cruiser plunged sharply beneath her feet as if an earthquake had struck. She snatched wildly at the railing, missed and fell into the harbour with a terrified shriek. A torrent of salt water poured into her mouth. Flailing wildly, she tried to fight her way back to the surface. Normally she was a good swimmer, but then she did not usually swim in a wedding-dress. The folds of material were rapidly filling up with water and dragging her down, the veil was wrapped tightly around her neck and her lungs felt ready to burst. One of her white satin shoes slipped off her foot and she kicked wildly, trying to free the other one. All around her there was nothing but an explosion of bubbles and green blurry water and inside her chest was the beginning of a searing pain. Suddenly strong arms appeared from nowhere and dragged her to the surface. She opened her mouth and took in a long, choking gulp of fresh air. Her wet veil felt like a strangling rope around her throat and she fought with a new vigour to try and free herself. Then to her relief the encumbrance was suddenly torn loose and flung away. Beth became aware that somebody's strong arm was flung over her left shoulder and holding her tightly under her right armpit. For an instant she lay motionless with relief in that reassuring grip. Then she saw her veil beginning to fill with water and sink beneath the green surface of the waves.

'Oh, no, my veil!' she gasped, struggling wildly to try and grab it. 'I can't lose that.'

'I'll buy you a new one,' promised a deep masculine voice.

Lean brown fingers thrust aside her wet curls and she caught a glimpse of keen dark eyes. Then her rescuer began to swim in a strong, effortless side-stroke, dragging her after him. Raising her head, she saw the gleaming white stern of a yacht dead ahead of them. When they reached it, the stranger shouted to somebody on board and a rope-ladder came splashing down into the water beside her. By now Beth was shivering with cold and shock and her first fumbling attempts to get a grip on the ladder were in vain. With an impatient oath the man in the water grabbed her by the back of her dress and hoisted her almost bodily over the stern of the yacht. A moment later he had hauled himself up beside her.

'Are you all right?' he demanded.

Beth opened her mouth to speak but was seized by a paroxysm of coughing. With an involuntary gulp she ducked her head over the rear of the yacht and was violently sick into the water.

As she straightened up, shuddering and gasping, she saw a sight that took her breath away. On the green surface of the water where the motor launch had been bobbing only moments before, there was nothing but a single red lifebelt surrounded by a few scraps of floating wreckage.

'What happened to our boat?' she demanded, her voice sharp with alarm.

'It sank,' replied her rescuer. 'And you're lucky you didn't go down with it.'

'But Warren and the photographer...where are they?'

Her voice was shrill with fear and the stranger grabbed her by the shoulders and turned her round to face the south.

'They've swum to the wharf,' he said. 'Don't worry, they look fine.' Beth followed his pointing finger to a spot where the grey outline of Stearns Wharf could be seen jutting out into the water. Sure enough, Warren and Michael had already climbed out on to the wooden planks of the wharf and were wringing the water out of their soaked clothing. As she watched, Warren turned and made an obscene gesture towards the yacht.

'You reckless, destructive bastard!' he shouted across the water. 'I'll sue you for this.'

'We'll see about that!' muttered the stranger grimly. 'Benson, take us ashore at the Yacht Club and phone the police.'

He turned back to Beth and held out his hand.

'My name is Daniel Pryor,' he said curtly.

Something in his manner was as threatening as if he were pointing a loaded gun at her. Yet, not knowing what else to do, she shook hands.

'I'm Beth Saxon,' she replied.

It seemed ridiculous to be standing there exchanging such formal greetings when they looked like a pair of typhoon victims. Beth's white high-heeled shoes had been lost, her sodden veil was somewhere at the bottom of the harbour and her beautiful dress was soaked with salt water. She stole a swift glance at her rescuer. He didn't look much better. His brown, curly hair lay damp and sleek against his head, and his white polo-shirt and white yachting shorts clung closely to his muscular frame. He was about thirty-five, with a hawk-like nose, dark eyes, a square jaw and a powerfully built physique, all of which seemed hauntingly familiar, although quite unknown to her. Although he was not conventionally handsome, Daniel Pryor was the kind of man who would always stand out in a crowd. The kind of man Beth instinctively distrusted.

The skin on the back of her neck rose in goose-bumps that had nothing to do with the cold, as she realised whom he reminded her of. Her sister Kerry's ex-husband Greg. A ruthless, irresistible sensualist who had swept her sister through four years of passion, excitement and misery before abandoning her for another woman. Involuntarily Beth stiffened as Daniel took her arm.

'You're cold. Go below to the cabin and dry yourself off,' he ordered brusquely. 'There's a bathrobe of mine down there that you can put on. And when we get ashore we'll see about having your dress dry-cleaned.'

Hating herself for the strange, fluttering thrill that his deep voice woke inside her, Beth obeyed without any argument. But, as she clambered awkwardly down the hatch in her wet dress, a maelstrom of confused feelings seethed inside her. Uppermost were shock and disbelief. This couldn't have happened! And yet it *had* happened or she wouldn't be here dripping a dark trail of sea-water along the carpeted floor. All the same, the reality of the accident still hadn't sunk in. She felt numb, as if she were watching a blurred video about someone else. Some girl who had nearly drowned. That thought made her stiffen in horror, recalling those terrifying moments underwater before Daniel Pryor had saved her. Once again she felt the urgent grip of his powerful arms, the way he had thrust her upwards to the life-giving air. And, in spite of her misgivings about his raw animal magnetism, relief and gratitude flooded through her.

But this was followed almost at once by more turbulent emotions. Fear, apprehension, confusion. Why did she have to be saved by a man who woke such uncomfortable memories in her? Nobody had ever known of Beth's unwilling attraction to her brother-in-law, because she had taken very good care that they shouldn't. And when Greg, with his brooding bedroom eyes and husky, caressing voice, had finally abandoned her sister, Beth had viewed his departure with relief. After all, his callous behaviour had simply confirmed her view that sexy men were likely to be incredibly dangerous and destructive. But that didn't make it any easier to cope with another one made in the same mould, especially when he appeared out of the blue like this. Not that she really knew anything about Daniel Pryor. Except that his arms were incredibly strong, his voice was like dark velvet and simply being in his presence made her feel weak at the knees. Yet that was quite enough to set alarm bells ringing in her head.

Beth shuddered as she gripped the cabin door-handle. One thing she was sure of—the sooner she was out of this situation, the better.

The cabin proved to be surprisingly luxurious in spite of its small size. The walls were upholstered in some kind of apricot-coloured vinyl and there was a large double bed with a grey and apricot cover. A strip of tiny lights ran along the cornice near the ceiling and stowage lockers were built into the walls. Pulling open a door, Beth saw that there was also a small *en-suite* bathroom decorated in pale green marble with a ceiling shaft to let in natural light from the deck above.

With shaking fingers she somehow managed to pull off the soaking wedding-dress and climbed into the shower. Two minutes under a refreshing downpour of hot water revived her spirits a little, but she was still too shaken to comprehend completely what had happened.

By the time she had dried off and wrapped a thick white towelling bathrobe around her she felt a bump as the yacht came alongside a jetty. Hastily rubbing her hair with the towel, she went into the cabin, opened one of the stowage lockers and looked inside. As she had hoped, she found a pair of leather thongs which she slipped on to her feet. A moment later there was a knock on the cabin door.

'Come in,' she called.

It was the man who had dragged her out of the water. Daniel Pryor. Unsmiling, soaking wet and with an expression of veiled exasperation on his face. And there was no mistaking the undertone of controlled hostility in his voice when he spoke.

'If you've finished, Miss Saxon,' he said, 'I'll just get changed myself and then we'll go ashore. Perhaps you'd like to wait for me up on deck.'

'Y-yes, of course,' stammered Beth. She looked around in a dazed fashion, caught sight of the wedding-dress still crumpled on the floor in the tiny bathroom. 'But my dress——'

'I'll bring it up with me when I come.'

Climbing up the hatchway on to the deck, she looked over the railings of the yacht and saw that they were drawn up alongside a jetty that formed part of the Yacht Club marina. And, to her alarm, she saw a policeman with a notebook standing at the far end of the jetty.

'Do you know what's going on?' she asked the short, grey-haired crewman who was sitting at the tiller of the yacht. His red, genial face wore an imperturbable look, as if collisions on the harbour were all in a day's work for him. But at Beth's question he unbent enough to smile faintly.

'Don't you worry, madam,' he replied in a clipped British accent. 'Mr Pryor will handle it, whatever it is.'

An almost reverent note crept into his voice as he spoke Daniel's name and Beth found herself unaccountably irritated by it. She longed desperately to escape from this situation, but there was little she could do except wait. After a couple of minutes Daniel Pryor emerged from the hatchway looking casually well dressed in short-sleeved grey and white striped shirt, matching grey shorts and rope-soled espadrilles. He handed a large plastic bag to Benson and turned to Beth. His face was impassive as he stretched out one hand to her.

'You'd better let me help you ashore,' he offered. 'You won't be able to climb very well in that outfit.'

Reluctantly Beth allowed him to take her arm and help her over the railing on to the jetty. An involuntary tingle sparked through her at the touch of his warm fingers and she broke away the moment she was safely ashore. To her dismay she saw that an interested knot of spectators was collecting near the clubhouse and watching as the policeman strolled towards them. He touched his cap in a brief gesture of respect.

'Sorry to trouble you, Mr Pryor,' he said pleasantly, 'but we've had a complaint laid that you rammed somebody out there in the bay.'

Daniel Pryor's dark eyes took on a stormy expression and his chin set into a hard line.

'Perhaps we can go inside the clubhouse and discuss the matter in private,' he said.

'Yes, sir,' agreed the policeman.

Beth scuffled along between them in her overlarge thongs, trying not to think about the disturbing responses which Daniel Pryor's nearness awoke in her. In any case, she had plenty of other problems to worry about. What really had happened out there in the bay? Had the motor launch really sunk so fast? And, if so, just whose fault was it? And what would happen to Warren if he was responsible?

Reaching the clubhouse, Daniel held open the door for her and ushered her inside. Then, after a quick word to an official, he led her into a private office along with the policeman.

'Please sit down, Officer,' he invited. 'But if you don't mind we'll make this as brief as possible. The young lady has an important appointment to keep.'

Beth's dark eyebrows met in a puzzled line. Do I? she thought. What appointment? But Daniel was already talking again. Striding across the room to a whiteboard that hung on one wall, he picked up a red felt pen and began drawing a diagram, while he explained rapidly what had happened. The conversation immediately became too technical for Beth to follow with its talk of port tacks, starboard tacks, figure-of-eights and wind directions. But the policeman was nodding attentively. In a few moments he closed his notebook with a snap and nodded with a satisfied expression.

'Seems like an open-and-shut case to me,' he said, standing up. 'Power gives way to sail, it's as simple as that.'

Beth rose uncertainly to her feet.

'Can I go, then?' she asked. 'Is it all over?'

A faint look of sardonic amusement crinkled the corners of Daniel Pryor's eyes. 'Were you afraid we were going to put you in gaol?' he asked. 'Yes, I'd say it's all over. Wouldn't you, Officer?'

'Yes, I would,' agreed the policeman. 'Unless that other guy wants to take you to court, but in my opinion that would be a plain stupid thing for him to do.'

'Do you know what's happened to him?' stammered Beth anxiously. 'Warren Clark, I mean, the man who was driving the motor launch. My fiancé. Are you sure he wasn't hurt?'

'Well, ma'am,' replied the policeman with a harassed expression, 'the last I saw of him, he was on his way down to the hospital to get himself checked out, but it didn't seem as if there was too much wrong with him. Now, if you'll excuse me, I'd better be going. I have other work to do.'

As the door closed behind him, Beth sank shakily into a chair. Delayed shock was beginning to assault her and her thoughts whirled crazily. I hope Warren's not hurt, she mused, but if he isn't why hasn't he come to find me? And where do I go from here?

'Hospital,' she echoed. 'What on earth do I do now?'

A faint tremor shivered through her limbs and she had to fight down the urge to fling herself into Daniel's arms and burst into tears. Oh, lord, she thought miserably. If he knew what I was thinking, I'd be so embarrassed, I'd curl up and die. Biting her lip, she darted Daniel a stricken glance and then lifted her head defiantly.

Daniel Pryor stood gazing at her for a moment out of brooding dark eyes, then the grim look around the corners of his mouth suddenly softened. Crossing the room, he laid his hand briefly on her shoulder. His touch seemed to scorch through the towelling bathrobe and Beth shifted uneasily, willing him not to notice the way her pulse-rate suddenly soared and her breathing grew fast and shallow. No doubt, with his aura of power and sensuality, women threw themselves at him all the time. But she had no desire to make a fool of herself. Chemistry, she thought cynically, that's all it is. And she tried to draw away from his touch.

Her movement attracted his attention. Panic jolted through her as she met that smouldering gaze and then glanced hastily away. She felt her cheeks flushing hotly and yearned for him to say something to ease the strain. But for several moments he remained thoughtfully silent. And, when he did speak, his voice had a harsh edge to it.

'Well, it's not your fault that you're engaged to an idiot,' he growled. 'And I can't help taking pity on a bride. So cheer up, Miss Saxon. I'm sure we can get you both to the church on time.'

Beth stared at him with a baffled expression.

'What are you talking about?' she demanded. 'What church?'

Daniel frowned, radiating a dose of antagonism that was as ominous and unmistakable as the massing of thunderclouds before a storm.

'To the church where you're getting married, of course,' he replied curtly. 'Which reminds me, you'd better give me some details. Where was the wedding supposed to be held and what time? Is there someone I should call to tell them you'll be late?'

Light suddenly dawned inside Beth's confused brain. She gave a half-hysterical gulp of laughter.

'There isn't any wedding,' she explained. 'We were just doing fashion photos and I was modelling the bridal dress. I'm not getting married today.'

The expression on his face baffled her. The thunderous scowl relaxed fractionally and was replaced by a look of fierce amusement.

'No wedding?' he drawled lazily. 'Well, that is interesting. In that case, I guess there's no real harm done, is there?'

A shadow crossed Beth's face and she took in breath in a long, shaky sigh. Dismissing her tumultuous reactions to Daniel as too dangerous to contemplate, she tried to focus on the consequences of the morning's events. Now that she knew Warren was safe, the other glaring result of the accident occurred to her.

'Oh, yes, there is,' she said miserably. 'If that motor launch has really sunk to the bottom of the harbour, then my entire collection of autumn clothes has gone with it. All except for the bridal gown, and that's probably ruined by the salt water.'

Daniel shrugged indifferently.

'Well, I wouldn't worry too much about that,' he said. 'Your insurance will cover the clothes. And you can easily buy some more right here in Santa Barbara.'

'But you don't understand,' protested Beth passionately, her voice rising and growing faster. 'I can't just go out to a shop and replace those! They were originals. Clothes that I designed and made myself. Each of those is one of a kind and I'm supposed to be displaying them at a fashion show in Los Angeles in three days' time. So now what am I going to do?' She broke off suddenly and her eyes filled with tears. 'It's the end of everything I've worked for!'

Daniel's harsh, brooding features took on an expression of total absorption, as if he were a chess master faced by a teasing problem or a champion skier embarking on a taxing downhill slalom.

'Where are you staying in Santa Barbara?' he rapped out.

Beth stared at him in bewilderment.

'Nowhere,' she said. 'Warren and I drove a hire car up here from Los Angeles during the night. And we were going to drive back this afternoon.'

'Right. That simplifies things. Where was your luggage? In the car?'

'No. All aboard the motor launch,' said Beth despairingly.

'Never mind. We'll replace it. Now we'd better get moving if we're going to sort this out. Come on.'

He dragged her to her feet, opened the door and thrust her out into the clubroom's main lounge.

'But where are you taking me?' demanded Beth.

'Back to my place to get things organised,' replied Daniel. He snapped his fingers at a figure who was hovering discreetly on the far side of the room. 'Benson, come here. I want you to go down town and buy Miss Saxon some clothes. A size eight, I'd say at a guess. And how about shoes? What size do you take?'

'Six,' stammered Beth, wondering whether her companion had gone right off his head.

'And size six shoes,' finished Daniel briskly. 'Enough for three days. Bring them back to the house as soon as possible.'

'Yes, sir,' replied Benson, turning on his heel and departing.

Daniel intercepted Beth's look of horrified disbelief and a mocking smile flickered suddenly around the edges of his mouth.

'Don't worry, Benson is a genuine English butler,' he assured her. 'And he has excellent taste. I'm sure you'll like the clothes he chooses.'

'It's not that!' wailed Beth. 'But you must see, I can't possibly go with you. I don't know anything about you.'

Daniel brushed aside this objection with a careless wave of his hand. 'I'm not really in the habit of kidnapping young women,' he assured her wearily. 'But I'm sure the Yacht Club manager will give me a character reference if you need it. Now, are you coming with me or not?'

Beth stared at him, feeling completely taken aback. She couldn't help feeling an ominous sense of misgiving about the prospect of going off with Daniel. Not that she expected him to do her any harm, but she sensed a subtler kind of danger in his company. The danger of an intoxicating, sensual attraction whose potency she could not ignore. Yet what else could she do? Alone in a strange city with no possessions, who else could she turn to? Besides, she need not stay long. If he would just let her use his phone to contact Warren, she could be on her way again as soon as Benson brought her some clothes.

'I suppose I'll have to,' she said slowly. 'I don't know where else I could go in your dressing-gown anyway.'

Daniel gave a low growl of laughter.

'Well, you could try getting a job as a mannequin in a store window,' he suggested. 'But failing that I think you'd better come home with me and have some breakfast.'

With a feeling of unreality Beth allowed herself to be led out into the car park and handed into a gleaming silver Jaguar. As they drove through the streets of Santa Barbara, she pinched herself quietly on the arm, wondering whether all of this was real. But the white Spanish-style buildings with their orange-tiled roofs, the tall palm trees with their waving fronds like giant pineapples, the dark blue soaring backdrop of the hills and the glimmering expanse of the harbour all looked much the same as they had an hour earlier.

'Where are you from?' asked Daniel abruptly. 'You don't sound like an American.'

'I'm not,' agreed Beth. 'I'm from Australia.'

'And what are you doing in California?' he asked. 'Are you on vacation?'

'No.' She shook her head and felt drips of water cascade down her neck. 'I'm here on business, or I was.'

'What kind of business? Fashion design?'

'Yes. I've been invited to show my autumn collection of clothes at a big fashion parade in Los Angeles on Tuesday.'

'Los Angeles, huh?' echoed Daniel. 'So what made you come to Santa Barbara? Are you just having a weekend off before the big event?'

Beth shook her head again, trying to fight off the despair that was beginning to well up inside her.

'No. We just drove up from Los Angeles to do some publicity photos of the collection. I couldn't afford a professional model, so I modelled the clothes myself.'

'What were the photos for?' asked Daniel. 'Advertising?'

'Yes, sort of. You see, after the fashion show on Tuesday there'll be trade shows in other places: New York, Miami, that sort of thing. What they do is hire a large hall and everyone sets up a booth with photos of their collection so buyers can come and see them and order whatever they want. I showed my clothes to an agent in LA and she encouraged me to get the photos done and send them on to New York. If the show went well on Tuesday, I was hoping I could break into the rest of the US market. But now——'

Her voice wobbled suddenly. She pressed the back of her hand to her mouth.

'I see,' said Daniel softly. 'But now your entire autumn collection is at the bottom of the Santa Barbara harbour and you think your life is ruined. Is that right?'

Beth's eyes blurred suddenly. Two large tears rolled down her cheek.

'That's about it,' she breathed huskily.

Daniel's powerful right hand shot out and squeezed her fingers so hard that she felt the bones grate. She glanced at him in surprise and his dark eyes met hers briefly in a look that seared her. Then he turned back to face the road, gritting his teeth as if he had just taken some momentous decision.

'Trust me,' he urged. 'I'll find a way to solve your problem.'

Beth gave a croaking laugh which was close to a sob.

'If you do, you're a magician!' she said bitterly. 'Anyway, why should you bother?'

'I have my reasons,' he said cryptically.

CHAPTER TWO

BETH was still puzzling over what he meant when the
road suddenly took a turn up into the hills and the car
began to climb along a series of winding lanes. At last
Daniel turned off the road at the imposing entrance to
a villa. Black wrought-iron gates rose eight feet high in
an intricate filigree pattern between two massive pillars
of honey-coloured stucco. On either side of the gateway
hung Spanish wrought-iron carriage-lamps. Beyond the
gates, Beth caught a glimpse of a garden which looked
cool and green and inviting. Amid its tangled foliage the
driveway curved out of sight in a dappled pattern of
light and shade.

Daniel touched a button on the sun visor above the
windscreen and with barely a squeak the gates swung
wide open. They drove through a twisting avenue of cypresses for nearly two hundred yards before at last the
house itself came into view. It was an imposing villa built
in a Spanish style with cream stuccoed walls, black
shutters, orange roof-tiles and a clock tower. Daniel
parked the Jaguar on a brick terrace and led Beth up to
the front entrance of the house. This too was in the
Spanish style with pillars of sandstone, an arched entranceway and double doors surmounted by a graceful
fanlight. In the centre of the porch hung another
wrought-iron lamp and on either side of the door there
were tubs of light blue lobelias and yellow violas to soften
the harshness of the sandstone.

Daniel inserted a key into the brass lock and flung
open the doors, revealing a cool marble-floored hallway.

On the right this gave way to an open-plan living and dining area with a parquetry floor, Mexican rugs, a lot of black leather and chrome furniture and a huge central fireplace stacked with freshly sawn logs. Most of the far wall was occupied by floor-to-ceiling glass French doors which led on to a shady terrace. Striding across the room, Daniel unlocked one of these doors and ushered Beth outside.

'Go and sit by the pool,' he urged, 'while I rustle up some breakfast.'

'Can I do anything to help?' asked Beth in a subdued voice.

'Yes. You can stop looking as if you're about to face an executioner at any moment,' replied Daniel.

But Beth found the advice hard to follow. Slumping into a garden chair, she cupped her chin in her hands and gazed moodily over the vista that lay before her. It was an attractive sight. Beyond the kidney-shaped pool was a brick terrace flanked by tubs of geraniums and bordered by a low wall. Below this the ground dropped away sharply to reveal a breathtaking view of the Pacific Ocean. By now the sun was high in the sky and the sea had turned a deep cobalt-blue. Huge, fluffy white clouds floated against a paler blue sky and the bright sunlight gleamed back from the creamy white stucco walls of the Spanish-style houses far below. Bees buzzed in the flowering plants that climbed a trellis on one wall and the air was sweet and heavy with the scent of jasmine.

It should have been a wonderful experience sitting here on this five-hundred-foot-high hilltop overlooking the ocean and surrounded by every imaginable luxury, but nothing could raise Beth's spirits at the moment. In the space of the last hour her world seemed to have fallen to pieces. Her fiancé Warren was off in some unnamed hospital, possibly injured. All her possessions were at the bottom of the Santa Barbara harbour and her bright hopes of breaking into American fashion design were in ruins. All she had were the clothes she stood up in and even those didn't belong to her. They belonged to that extraordinary American who had whisked her away to his hilltop hideaway and who seemed to be quite out of touch with reality. And why had Daniel invited her here? A tremor of anxiety skittered through her as she tried to fathom his motives. Was he planning to try and seduce her? Beth was no fool and she couldn't help suspecting that the current of tingling physical awareness which had sparked between them at the Yacht Club had stung Daniel as fiercely as her. Yet she couldn't keep running away from physically alluring men for the rest of her life just because of one bad experience. Besides, sparks of sexual attraction must ignite beween people all the time and it didn't necessarily stop them from having any social contacts. She would simply have to remain cool and aloof and hope that Daniel did likewise. All the same, she couldn't help feeling profoundly disturbed by being here.

Turning in her chair, she looked back towards the house and saw that the kitchen also faced on to the terrace. Through the window she could see Daniel grinding coffee and simultaneously holding an animated conversation on a mobile telephone which was tucked into the crook of his shoulder. Catching her eye, he winked at her. A heady feeling of excitement rushed through her veins, then she sighed and sank further down into her chair with her shoulders hunched. This is crazy, she thought to herself. What on earth am I doing here?

Ten minutes later Daniel appeared on the terrace carrying a tray loaded with hot blueberry muffins, coffee, orange juice and butter. To Beth's astonishment the mobile phone was also sitting on the tray.

'Right, let's eat and then we'll solve your problem.'

Beth gave him a glum look but accepted a hot muffin and a cup of coffee. Despite her depression the strong, sweet coffee and the tart, crumbly muffins began to revive her. For the first time she felt capable of looking ahead more than the next five minutes. And something occurred to her which had not yet crossed her mind. Wincing, she decided to get the uncomfortable moment over with.

'I'm awfully sorry about the accident,' she blurted out. 'I hope your yacht didn't suffer too much damage, but, if it did, I want you to know that we'll pay. Somehow.'

'Forget my yacht!' he said roughly. 'If your insurance doesn't cover it, mine certainly will. And we've more important matters to discuss. Now are you ready to make plans?'

She bit her lip and nodded.

'I guess so. And the first thing I'd better do is find out which hospital Warren's at and let him know that I'm OK.'

'That's already taken care of,' Daniel assured her swiftly. 'I phoned and checked. Warren's at the Mater Hospital. He's perfectly fine and he knows that you're here.'

'Thank you,' sighed Beth. 'In that case I suppose he'll be arriving any time now to collect me.'

'Maybe,' retorted Daniel. 'But I can't help finding it pretty damned strange that he ever left you in the first place. If you'd been my fiancée, I'd have wanted to know that you were OK immediately. What I'd like to know is why the hell he didn't come to the Yacht Club to look for you.'

Beth fought down a disloyal temptation to wonder the same thing. Adroitly she changed the subject.

'You know, I think I'll have to accept your offer of those clothes you sent Benson to buy,' she said hastily. 'After all, I can't go back to Los Angeles in your bathrobe or in a wet wedding-gown. But if you write down your address for me I'll make sure that you're repaid. And if you could just phone the hospital and remind Warren to pick me up I'd be very grateful.'

'Don't be ridiculous,' said Daniel sternly. 'You're not going anywhere. We've got to find a way of getting your fashion collection ready for the show on Tuesday.'

Beth gave a gasp of astonished laughter.

'That's impossible!' she cried. 'Look, I'm sure you mean well, but I don't believe there's any way we can get those clothes back off the bottom of the harbour.'

Daniel nodded tranquilly and buttered a muffin.

'No, you're right there,' he agreed. 'I already phoned a diving and salvage firm while I was in the kitchen and they said the same thing, so I guess you'll just have to make a new lot of clothes.'

Beth groaned.

'A new lot of clothes?' she echoed incredulously. 'You must be joking! It would take half a dozen dressmakers working round the clock for the next six days to reproduce those clothes. There's no way I could get a new collection together by Tuesday.'

'Is that right?' asked Daniel, setting down his muffin and reaching for the mobile phone. He punched in some numbers. 'Let me see, six dressmakers working round the clock for six days? Well, that shouldn't be too difficult. Hello? Wendy? Listen, I need two dozen dressmakers to come over to my place right away and work round the clock until Monday night. Can you do that?'

Beth watched aghast as Daniel nodded, smiled and wrote down a couple of figures on a small notepad. Then he switched off the phone.

'It's all settled,' he said tranquilly. 'They'll be round in an hour.'

Beth stared at him in horror.

'Do you seriously mean to tell me you just hired two dozen dressmakers to make up my clothes for the show on Tuesday?' she demanded.

Daniel nodded.

'You've got it,' he agreed.

'But I can't possibly afford that!' cried Beth. 'All I have in the world is two hundred dollars in a bank account in Sydney and the clothes I stand up in. And even those belong to you.'

'Don't worry. I'll foot the bill,' Daniel assured her.

'But why should you put money into solving my problems?'

'I'm an entrepreneur,' he replied with a shrug. 'I often put up capital for deserving business ventures. And what could be more deserving than a bride in distress? Anyway, you can pay me back once you're rich and famous.'

Beth felt an uncomfortable sensation in her stomach, as if she had just plunged three floors in a lift.

'What if I never am rich and famous?' she demanded.

Daniel's white teeth flashed in a taunting smile.

'Then I guess I'll just have to sue you for my bathrobe,' he replied.

Beth twisted her fingers together nervously.

'Look, this may be a big joke to you,' she said. 'But it's really important to me. I appreciate your offer, but what you're trying to do is impossible. Besides, I just can't afford to get into that kind of debt.'

Or get involved with a man who attracts me so much, she added silently. Daniel stirred his coffee and raised one eyebrow.

'Funny,' he remarked. 'You don't look like the kind to just give up and die. I thought you had guts.'

Beth's blue eyes blazed. She knew her faults as well as anyone, but she never gave up on anything that mattered. Even her mother said she was stubborn.

'I'm not just giving up and dying!' she cried defiantly. 'And I do have guts. But what you're trying to do is ridiculous!'

'Is it?' asked Daniel softly. His dark eyes scanned her face, issuing a challenge which she could not ignore. 'Or is it just that you don't have the courage to go for broke? Come on, Beth, couldn't those twenty-four women reproduce the collection in three days under your guidance? It's twice as many as you said you'd need. Couldn't they, if you really put your heart and soul into it and refused to be defeated?'

Beth hesitated, feeling her cheeks stain with colour. An unwilling surge of mingled terror and exultation flooded through her.

'I—I suppose so,' she stammered. 'In theory. But it's not really practical. I'd need all kinds of equipment, sewing machines, scissors, everything...'

'That's easy,' said Daniel, reaching for the phone again. 'I'll just call up and order what you need.'

Impulsively Beth reached out and gripped his powerful brown hand.

'Please don't,' she begged. 'You're just getting me in deeper and deeper and I know I'll never be able to repay you. This is all moving much too fast for me.'

Daniel shook off her hand.

'Look, honey,' he growled. 'I was a movie producer and director in Hollywood for ten years and in that business there's only the quick and the dead. Trust me. I know what I'm doing. Now, what do you need?'

Sinking back into her chair, Beth stared at him with a defeated expression. Arguing with Daniel Pryor was obviously like trying to swim the wrong way up Niagara

Falls or scratch your way through solid rock with your bare fingernails. You could do nothing but lose. With a strong feeling of unreality and the first fluttering pangs of excitement she picked up his Biro and notepad and began to make a list.

'A dozen sewing machines,' she said. 'Dressmakers' dummies, cutting boards, scissors, pins, lots of coloured threads, chalk...'

Daniel's eyes narrowed in amusement.

'There,' he said. 'It's not so painful, is it? And you won't even need to do any of the sewing yourself. These women have all worked as wardrobe mistresses in Hollywood. They're the best there is. All you'll have to do is tell them what you want.'

A fresh wave of panic washed over Beth.

'But I don't know how to tell anyone what to do,' she protested. 'I've never done this kind of thing before. I've always had to do all the work myself except for a little bit of help from Warren. I wouldn't know where to begin with bossing people around.'

'Then you'd better learn fast,' ordered Daniel crisply. 'I'd say your career is on the verge of taking off like a rocket. So I suggest you just hang on and enjoy the ride.'

Twenty minutes later Daniel's valet, Benson, arrived back from the city with half a dozen carrier bags full of clothes, far more that Beth would ever have thought necessary for a three-day period. Daniel picked up the bags and led her through to the guest wing where he showed her into a vast bedroom decorated in Spanish style. Dropping the bags unceremoniously on the bed, he looked at his watch.

'Be as quick as you can,' he warned. 'Wendy and the girls will be here soon.'

When the door had closed behind him, Beth emptied the bags out on to the bed. Her eyes opened wide in amazement. Benson had bought enough clothes for a three-month holiday rather than a three-day working stint. There was hand-embroidered French underwear, three cotton nightdresses, a bikini, shorts, T-shirts, half a dozen pairs of shoes ranging from blue trainers to black evening shoes, a tracksuit, a dressing-gown, three day-dresses and a smart business suit in pale blue linen. In addition a waterproof bag held a selection of toiletries and make-up. Shaking her head in disbelief, Beth chose a pair of blue and yellow checkered shorts with a matching pale blue top and leather sandals.

When she was dressed, she took the expensive hair-brush from the toiletries bag and brushed her blonde curls into some kind of order. Then, staring at herself thoughtfully in the huge mirror above the dressing-table, she applied some make-up. A light beige foundation, a hint of blusher on her cheeks, a coral-pink lipstick and a touch of blue eyeshadow to bring out the colour of her eyes. 'I'll bet this is the weirdest "wedding-day" anyone ever had,' she muttered to herself.

Just at that moment there was a knock at the door and she hurried to answer it. It was Daniel.

'Are you ready, Beth?' he asked. 'Wendy and the girls are here.'

She followed him along the hallway, her sandals scuffing lightly on the brown terracotta tiles. Turning a corner, he flung open a door and revealed a spacious ballroom more than forty feet long. Beth's mouth fell open at the scene of frantic activity that faced her. On the opposite side of the room the French doors were open and two workmen in blue overalls were staggering in, carrying a heavy sewing cabinet. Eight or nine other sewing cabinets were already set up along the room and some of them already had sewing machines in place. At the far end of the room a woman with ginger hair was pushing a couple of full-sized mirrors on castors into place. Next to them was a noticeboard covered in black hessian. The hum of conversation was reverberating around the room, but Daniel raised his voice above the uproar and addressed the woman with the ginger hair.

'Wendy, could you come here, please? I want you to meet Beth.'

The woman turned round and her homely features split into a wide smile. She was covered with freckles as heavily as if they had been sprinkled on with a chocolate shaker. Her purple shorts and top were already festooned with the tools of her trade. A tape measure hung around her neck and a wrist pin-cushion studded with bright red and yellow and blue pins was attached firmly to her left wrist. She hurried across the room to meet them, both hands outstretched.

'Oh, Daniel!' she cried. 'This is the most exciting thing that's happened to me in weeks. Hi, Beth, how are you? I'm Wendy Fulton. Now, what do you want us to do?'

Hesitantly Beth began to explain. In a moment Wendy interrupted her to find a sketch-book and some coloured pencils. Beth sat down and began to draw and talk at the same time, with a sense of rising excitement. Was it really possible that they might achieve this incredible feat? Her eyes met Daniel's and he gave her a faint smile. She caught her breath and then smiled back at him uncertainly.

'Just call Blair's down in the city if you need any fabric sent up,' he told Wendy. 'I'll be in my study if you need me. And make sure this young lady gets some sleep some time tonight, won't you?'

And with that he slipped away.

Beth had never worked so hard in all her life. Nor had she ever known that work could be so exhilarating. For the next few hours she was so busy that she scarcely had time to breathe. Under her direction the twelve women traced out patterns, cut fabrics and sewed together garments with a speed that amazed and enthralled her. And as the day wore on her secret conviction that Daniel Pryor was stark raving mad slowly began to give way to the wild hope that he might be a genuine miracle-worker. By seven o'clock in the evening, when the second shift of dressmakers came on duty, several garments were already completed. And more were laid out in pieces on the floor or pinned to the dressmakers' dummies. When Benson came into the ballroom to announce that dinner was being served in the dining-room, Beth was too excited to join the others.

'I'll just stay on here and keep working,' she said. 'I'm really not hungry but if you could send me in something to drink I'd be grateful.'

Ten minutes later the English butler returned with a glass of lemon mineral water, a toasted chicken sandwich and salad on a tray. Beth smiled warmly at him, gulped down the mineral water and left the sandwich for a moment while she went to check on some problems. For the rest of the evening time flew by as she cut out fabric, drew coloured sketches or hovered anxiously behind the sewing machines, directing the workers. At the back of her mind she noted absently that Benson had switched on the overhead lights and that the garden outside was growing dark, but she was absolutely stunned when a sudden burst of laughter in the corridor outside the room announced the return of the first shift of workers. The ginger-haired Wendy came back into the room and stopped dead with a reproving clicking of her tongue.

'Oh, Beth!' she exclaimed reproachfully. 'Are you still here? Don't you realise it's three o'clock in the morning?'

'What?' cried Beth. 'I don't believe you.'

She was crouching on the floor over a cutting-board and, as she tried to rise to her feet, a sudden cramp locked the muscles of her leg so that she had to hobble around painfully, squealing and massaging her calf. Wendy gave an exasperated groan and came to her aid.

'Daniel will be furious if he hears that you've been running yourself as hard as this,' she said. 'Come on, sit down for a minute, honey, and let me massage it. When did you last eat?'

'I don't know,' said Beth vaguely, giving a low gasp of pain as Wendy kneaded the cramped muscle. 'I had a chicken sandwich earlier on.'

Wendy's glance tracked across the room to the plate containing a large toasted sandwich with a single bite taken out of it.

'Oh, did you?' she demanded drily.

Beth grinned, showing fugitive dimples. 'Well, I meant to,' she said. 'Oh, that leg is much better. Thank you, Wendy.'

Wendy hauled her to her feet. 'Look, why don't you go to bed now?' she demanded. 'You look really bushed.'

'I know,' admitted Beth ruefully. 'But I can't bear to leave until I know that suede jacket is safely finished. That's the one I'm really praying over.'

Wendy took her arm and propelled her firmly towards the door. 'Well, if you won't go to bed, at least lie down in the conservatory for a while. And take some fresh food from the kitchen with you. I'll come and call you when the jacket's done.'

Beth stretched, feeling the ache in her shoulder and conscious of the sudden throbbing in her head. 'All right, I think I will,' she agreed.

Ten minutes later she ambled wearily into the back of the house and uttered a soft exclamation of delight. The room covered the full width of the house and was illu-

minated by concealed lighting hidden among the plants.
As Beth pressed the light switch, a soft golden glow filled
the entire room, revealing a luxuriant jungle of plants.
There were huge tubs of tuberous begonias, pink and
white and yellow. Baskets filled with trailing blue lobelias
hung from the ceiling and the walls were lined with
thickets of mauve hydrangeas. Every gap was filled with
the brilliantly coloured foliage of coleus plants, pink and
yellow and amazing shades of burgundy. The air was
heavy with the scent of lilies and somewhere she could
hear the sound of running water. Investigating further,
Beth found a little grotto tucked away in one corner
looking almost like a natural rock pool with its delicate
ferns and mosses and a fountain rippling into a pool
filled with goldfish.

'Oh, how nice,' she breathed, sinking into a con-
veniently placed chaise-longue and pulling up a bamboo
table. She had been too tired to make herself a fresh
meal, but she drank some lemonade straight from a can
and ate the remains of her chicken sandwich and the
salad. A large slice of Black Forest cake made a delicious dessert and she was asleep even before she had
finished licking the last smear of chocolate from her
fingers. How long she slept she didn't know, but she
dreamt that Warren was lifting her and carrying her
away, except that in the dream Warren was far stronger
and more tender than he had ever been in real life. It
was only when her bare legs brushed against a damp
hydrangea, spilling a shower of cold droplets over her
skin, that she came awake with a start and realised that
it was not Warren who was holding her. It was Daniel
Pryor. With a startled gasp she tried to struggle free.

'What are you doing?' she demanded. 'Put me down!'

He did as she asked, but did not release her. His left
arm remained tensed around her body, supporting her,

and she could not help being disturbingly conscious of his nearness and warmth. Panic jolted through her and she tried urgently to twist away.

'What's wrong?' he asked in a puzzled voice. 'Are you still dreaming? You look terrified.'

His arm tightened around her.

'No!' she choked. 'I'm not. I'm awake! It's just that...'

She paused and a shudder went through her. How could she possibly admit to herself, much less to him, that his mere presence was sheer torment to her? She inhaled sharply, feeling her senses swim at the spicy scent of his aftershave, mingled with the subtle aromas of the conservatory. Against the dark outlines of the plants his body seemed to loom over her, huge, primitive, vaguely threatening. And yet mysteriously she felt drawn to him so powerfully that her heart accelerated and her breathing grew fast and shallow. Her eyes dilated in alarm as he stepped towards her.

'It's all right,' he murmured soothingly. 'You've just woken in a strange place and lost your bearings. But you're quite safe. Trust me.'

His hands moved up and gripped her shoulders, kneading the tense muscles until she gave a soft groan and relaxed under his touch. Swaying slightly, she let herself rest against him. It felt wonderful to rest her head against his chest and let go of all her exhaustion and worry. But that momentary weakness was her undoing. As her cheek brushed against his shirt, she heard him catch his breath. Sleepily she looked up at him and their eyes met. She saw that he was watching her with a passionate urgency that both thrilled and appalled her. His intense, searing scrutiny took her breath away and she dropped her gaze, but her entire body still seemed to throb with awareness of him. Dizzy with longing, she sensed the exact way that his chin was brushing against the top of her head, his breath was fanning her hair and his hard, warm chest was pressed against her cheek. He was taller than Warren and more powerfully built, with massive shoulders and lean, muscular thighs. Yet it wasn't just his physique that set him apart from Warren, it was the air of power and authority that radiated out from him. Insanely, Beth wondered what it would be like to be kissed by a man like that. Darting him a fleeting, troubled glance, she tried half-heartedly to break away, and a moment later she had her answer.

With a muffled oath he caught her against him, holding her so tightly that she could feel his furiously beating heart. Then his lips came down on hers with a passion that shocked and enthralled her. Never had she been kissed like this, and she responded as if she had been born for this moment. His kisses were violent and devouring, as if he wanted to possess her, body and soul. Yet they awoke an answering need deep inside her and she kissed him back with equal frenzy. Glorying in his arrogant male strength and power, she arched her back and swayed sinuously against him. Her eyelids fluttered closed and her lips parted in a quivering invitation. Flame seemed to leap through every cell of her body at his urgent, demanding touch. And when he hauled her against him so hard that she could not mistake his fierce masculine arousal she gave a soft whimper deep in her throat. With an answering groan, he buried his face in her hair and nuzzled her sensually. Tremors of excitement prickled through her body as his lips travelled down the column of her throat in a trail of feather-light kisses. She shuddered, unable to bear the exquisite torment and yet wishing it would go on forever. In that moment their entire being seemed to melt and flow together in pure paradise.

'You're so beautiful,' Daniel murmured hoarsely. 'I feel I want to drown in your sweetness.'

The words were like a dash of cold water in her face. Jerking herself free, Beth stepped back a pace. The memory of Greg with his honeyed tongue and dark, caressing eyes rose like a spectre to haunt her.

'Leave me alone!' she cried, backing away from him. 'I'm not some gullible teenager to be taken in by a smooth line. Save your flattery for someone else!'

And, turning blindly away, she made a rush for the door. He caught her before she reached it and seized her by the wrist. Not hard, but with enough force to make her miserably sure that he was in control.

'What is this all about?' he demanded, his dark eyebrows drawing into a threatening frown. 'Would you mind telling me what's going on?'

Her breath came in fast, shallow gulps.

'Nothing is going on!' she hissed. 'That's the whole point. This should never have happened and, if you've any decency at all, you'll act as if it didn't. Please!'

And with a desperate lunge she broke away from him and fled.

CHAPTER THREE

IF BETH hadn't been so exhausted, she would have lain awake for hours worrying about what had happened in the conservatory. As it was, she simply crawled into bed and fell asleep the moment her head hit the pillow, but when she woke up the following morning she had an ominous feeling of misgiving, as if she were about to face final exams or a trip to the dentist. Pulling herself upright in the huge bed, she blinked around at the unfamiliar room and memory came hurtling back to her.

'Oh, no,' she groaned, sinking down under the covers. 'What on earth have I done?'

Her own behaviour the previous evening completely baffled her. She wasn't in the habit of kissing strange men. In fact she had never even had a serious boyfriend apart from Warren. So how on earth had she found herself swept into that passionate embrace with Daniel Pryor? Had he simply taken advantage of her exhaustion and shock to kiss her against her will? She gave a low, bitter laugh. No, that wasn't fair. It hadn't been against her will, she had been entirely willing and that was what alarmed her most. She had always been reserved and serious by nature, so much so that the other students at technical college had nicknamed her the Ice Maiden. But there had been nothing cold about the way she had melted into Daniel's embrace last night. Even thinking about it made a strange, tremulous warmth uncoil deep inside her.

The trouble was that the man had a kind of raw animal magnetism that ought to be banned by law. With his

wide shoulders and narrow hips, sultry dark eyes and
that faint brooding smile, he was a menace to any woman
between the ages of eight and eighty. After watching her
sister's tempestuous marriage come to grief, Beth had
never thought she would fall for something as primitive
as mere sex appeal. And the way she had responded to
Daniel the previous evening made her feel enormously
guilty. After all, she loved Warren, didn't she? Although
there had been moments in the last year or so when she
had wondered about that. Yet she had always hoped that
she and Warren would eventually be married, so how
could she ever have become so recklessly carried away
with somebody else?

The telephone rang beside her bed, interrupting her
reverie. She picked up the receiver and heard Benson's
brisk English tones on the other end of the line.

'Good morning, Miss Saxon. I trust you slept well.
I'm just calling to say that Mr Pryor would like you to
join him on the terrace for breakfast at ten o'clock.'

'Ten o'clock?' echoed Beth aghast. 'What's the time
now then?'

'Nine thirty-five, madam.'

'Oh, no,' groaned Beth. 'I'd meant to be downstairs
working with the girls by six o'clock. Look, please tell
Mr Pryor I'm sorry but I can't possibly meet him. I'll
just get some toast and tea in the kitchen and get back
to work.'

Benson cleared his throat apologetically.

'I regret to inform you, Miss Saxon, that Mr Pryor
was most insistent that you should join him and he certainly won't allow you back in the workroom before
eleven.'

Beth gave a gasp of incredulous laughter.

'What do you mean, he won't allow me?' she demanded. 'What's going to happen if I do go down there?'

'I have been instructed to act as a . . . "bouncer" is the term, I believe, madam.'

Beth choked with outraged amusement. What was Daniel Pryor—some kind of caveman? The order was ludicrous, but there was no point getting involved in an undignified argument with the butler about it.

'All right, Benson,' she sighed. 'I can't argue with that. I'll be on the terrace at ten o'clock.'

Climbing out of bed, she showered and dressed. Although she told herself that she had no urge to impress Daniel Pryor, she hesitated for a long time over her choice of clothes. Finally she decided on a jersey suit of pale blue and white with culottes and a matching top and she took special care over her make up and blow-drying her hair. She told herself that this was only to give her confidence for a difficult interview, but secretly she knew that there was more to it than that. She was surprised and rather touched to find that Benson had included a large vial of Ma Griffe scent in her toiletry bag. Taking off the cap, she sprayed a small jet of it on to her wrists and neck and then inhaled the elusive fragrance. Her stomach churned nervously. Oh, dear, she thought. I'm not looking forward to seeing Daniel again, but I suppose the only way to get over it is to confront it.

When she arrived on the terrace she found that it was another glorious Californian day filled with bright sunlight and the sound of birdsong from the garden. Daniel was lounging at a table on the terrace reading a newspaper but he rose to his feet as she approached. Her expert eye took in the details of his clothing and noted that he was wearing beige designer trousers and a blue and beige Pierre Cardin shirt with Gucci shoes. She was also uncomfortably aware that she hadn't underestimated his virile attraction the night before.

'Sit down,' he invited. 'And help yourself to some food.'

There was a vast array of dishes on the table. A frosted glass platter held wedges of luscious green honeydew melon, fresh pineapple, papaw and strawberries. Next to this was a hotplate from which came the enticing aroma of crispy bacon, grilled sausages and tomatoes. There was also a wicker basket full of mouthwatering Danish pastries, large jugs of orange and apple juice and a percolator of fresh coffee.

To cover her embarrassment Beth helped herself to a plate of fruit salad and began to eat, darting Daniel nervous glances. But he seemed totally unaware of either her embarrassment or the possible cause of it.

'So how did you get into fashion design?' he asked, laying aside his newspaper.

Beth was grateful for the neutral topic and began to babble rapidly.

'Well, my mother worked in a factory as a machinist when I was a little girl,' she said. 'We weren't very well off so she always had to make her own clothes at home. She brought home scraps of fabric from the factory and I used to help her. I really loved it. Sometimes the pieces of material were so small it needed a lot of ingenuity to put them together into a garment.'

Daniel's eyebrows rose.

'That sounds like a rather deprived childhood,' he remarked.

'Don't you dare say that!' exclaimed Beth indignantly. 'I may have been deprived of material things, but my mother is a really warm, affectionate person. I was never deprived of love and that's the most important thing.'

His lips twitched.

'I couldn't agree more,' he said. 'But you were quite poor, were you?'

'Yes, we were. My father had an accident on a building site when I was seven years old and was crippled by it. He didn't get much in compensation and my mother had three children and no real job training, so we couldn't help being poor.'

Her defiant tone bought a glint of amusement to Daniel's dark eyes.

'It's not a crime,' he murmured.

'You'd think it was the way some people talk,' retorted Beth. 'Warren always——'

She broke off, biting her lip.

'Warren always what?' asked Daniel.

'Never mind.'

He frowned and stroked his chin thoughtfully. But when he spoke again he said nothing about Warren.

'All right, so you helped make clothes when you were a little kid. Then what?'

'I did dressmaking at high school and won a scholarship to go to technical college. I spent three years there and in my final year I won the big prize for designing. It was a trip to London for the spring shows, which was wonderful. That was when I knew that I really wanted to be a fashion designer more than anything else in the world.'

Daniel nodded.

'I see. And how long ago was that?' he asked.

'Two years ago. When I came back I had to find a job, so I've been working in a big department store as a fashion buyer for the last two years and doing my designing at night.'

'And where does Warren come into all this? asked Daniel.

'He was in my fashion design course at technical college,' replied Beth. 'He dropped out in his last year, because he didn't get his assignments finished on time. But it didn't matter so much for him. His parents own a big chain of fashion stores and he was able to get a job right away.'

Daniel drank some more coffee and gritted his teeth as if it were bitter. 'Do you really intend to marry him?'

Beth gave him a flustered look. What business was it of his?

'I don't know,' she stammered warily. 'I hope so.'

'Are you sleeping with him?' he asked.

Her face flamed. 'I don't see that that's any business of yours,' she retorted.

'It might be,' he said cryptically. 'Anyway, let's just say I'm curious. Are you sleeping with him?'

Beth was silent for a moment, too angry to speak, and then it occurred to her that perhaps this was the best way of fending Daniel off once and for all. After all, she didn't want any more encounters like the one in the conservatory last night.

'Yes, I am,' she snapped.

His face remained impassive.

'I see. And what sort of business relationship do you have?'

She set her lips stubbornly. But his eyes remained fixed on her so piercingly that she felt that he was looking right into her soul.

'What difference does it make?' she muttered at last.

'I think I'm entitled to ask,' he replied evenly. 'Seeing that I'm backing you in this little venture to get your fashion collection together.'

She ground her teeth, unable to deny the truth of that.

'Well, we don't have any kind of formal partnership at this stage,' she admitted grudgingly. 'And I did most of the designs and the sewing for the collection, but Warren did help me now and then.'

'And whose name is it appearing under at the show?' asked Daniel.

'Both our names,' muttered Beth.

'Louder,' prompted Daniel.

'Both our names,' shouted Beth.

Daniel smiled unpleasantly. 'I see, he said. 'He takes advantage of you every which way he can, doesn't he?'

'And what's that supposed to mean?' asked Beth in a dangerous voice.

Daniel gave a mirthless laugh.

'That would be obvious to you, sweetheart,' he said, 'if you weren't so wet behind the ears. The guy is obviously sleeping with you without any intention of ever marrying you. And he's also using your talent and hard work to get himself ahead in business. If you had any brains at all, you'd give him the boot.'

'Don't talk about Warren like that!' protested Beth indignantly.

Daniel's lips drew back into a contemptuous sneer.

'Why not?' he demanded. 'It's obvious he's just using you. Besides, if your precious Warren is so concerned about you, why hasn't he come here to find you yet?'

Beth flushed uncomfortably. The same thought had crossed her own mind, although she certainly wasn't going to admit that to Daniel.

'Maybe he didn't get your message,' she suggested.

'Or maybe he's waiting for you to come running back to him like a devoted little puppy-dog,' he countered. 'Why don't you open your eyes to him, Beth? He's not going to come looking for you. He obviously doesn't care a damn about you.'

Beth flinched.

'He does care,' she insisted doggedly. 'And he will come. I'm sure he will.'

At that moment Benson appeared on the terrace with a discreet cough.

'Excuse me, sir,' he said. 'There's a Mr Warren Clark waiting for you in the den. He says he wants to speak to you both.'

Beth shot Daniel a triumphant look and felt a thrill of malicious pleasure at seeing him momentarily disconcerted.

'All right, we'll come and see what he wants,' he said.

When they entered the den, Warren was standing with one elbow propped on the mantelpiece and his back to the door, but he turned at the sound of their footsteps. He was only of medium height, but his body was so gracefully proportioned that he seemed taller. He was extremely handsome in an almost effeminate way, with toffee-brown eyes and long silky brown hair that was cut in two layers so that a long curtain of it kept falling forward over his face. Privately Beth had never much liked the style, since it meant that Warren had to continually push his hair back from his forehead with a flicking movement of his head. He did so now. There was no mistaking the displeasure in his face.

'What the hell are you doing here, Beth?' he demanded without preamble.

Beth opened her mouth to speak, but found herself foiled by Daniel who immediately took control of the situation.

'Sit down, Beth,' he ordered with a hint of steel in his voice. And he turned to Warren, his dark eyes narrowed and his face unsmiling. 'My name is Daniel Pryor. I guess you've come here to apologise for the accident yesterday.'

'No, I haven't!' grated Warren indignantly. 'You're the one who rammed me. And let me tell you, you're going to pay for it, pay dearly.'

'Is that so?' purred Daniel. 'Well, it seems to me, Mr Clark, your manners are about as poor as your sea-manship. I don't know if you're aware of it, but the law quite clearly states that a boat under power must always give way to a boat under sail. I was sailing into the harbour and it was your responsibility to give way to me. You were the one who caused the accident.'

Warren thrust out his chin aggressively.

'Now just a damn minute——' he began, stepping closer to Daniel.

Hastily Beth placed herself between them and laid one hand on the sleeve of Warren's Paisley shirt.

'He's right, Warren,' she said nervously. 'That's exactly what the policeman at the Yacht Club said. The accident was all our fault.'

Warren looked at her as if she had gone mad.

'Don't be such a fool, Beth,' he exclaimed in a low, urgent voice. 'You should never make an admission of liability like that.'

Beth's eyebrows met in a bewildered frown.

'Even when you're in the wrong?' she demanded.

'Especially when you're in the wrong,' insisted Warren.

Daniel's lips curled into a smile of sardonic amusement.

'What a pity you didn't go into law,' he murmured. 'I can see you would have been a great asset to the legal profession. But since you didn't, I think we'll leave our attorneys to argue the rights and wrongs of the case and decide on an appropriate settlement. I'll give you my card.'

He crossed the room to a handsome mahogany desk and withdrew a square of white cardboard which he handed to Warren. Warren held it between his finger and thumb as if he were juggling a scorpion.

'I get it,' he sneered. 'You think you're going to sue me and make big bucks out of me, don't you, Pryor? Well, you're wrong, because I'll hire the finest lawyer I can find. You might think you're just dealing with some nobody of a student. But I'm more important than you realise. I'm——'

'Oh, stop blustering, Warren!' cried Beth in exasperation. 'There's no need for all this sabre-rattling. Accidents do happen and there's no point being unpleasant about it.'

'Don't blame him,' murmured Daniel provocatively. 'He was probably born unpleasant.'

Warren's face turned white with rage.

'Why did you ever get involved with this arrogant bastard?' he demanded, turning to Beth.

Beth shot Daniel an exasperated glance. At the moment she was tempted to wonder the same thing herself, but her innate honesty forced her to be fair.

'He's been very kind to me since our launch sank yesterday,' she insisted.

'And what exactly is that supposed to mean?' asked Warren suspiciously.

'Sit down and I'll tell you,' begged Beth. 'You know how our clothing collection was lost when the launch sank? Well, Daniel has hired two dozen dressmakers to replace the entire collection in time for the show on Monday.'

Warren stared at her, open-mouthed.

'That's ridiculous!' he protested. 'It's impossible.'

'I know,' agreed Beth. 'That's what I thought at first, too. But it's happening, Warren. They've already finished seven or eight garments. Why don't you come and see? Why don't you stay here and help us? You'd be wonderful. You know what all the garments are supposed to look like and you could help me draft the patterns.'

Warren rose to his feet with a look of revulsion on his face and paced across the room.

'Stay here?' he echoed in disbelief.

'Yes! Some of the women are from out of town and they're sleeping right here in the house. They work eight hours on and eight hours off. Daniel's provided beds, meals, everything.'

There was a long, ominous silence.

'I see,' said Warren in a voice filled with meaning. 'And where exactly are you sleeping, Beth?'

'Right here,' stammered Beth. 'In one of the guest bedrooms.'

Warren laughed. A harsh, unpleasant sound.

'Oh, yes,' he agreed. 'One of the guest bedrooms, for now. But it won't be long before it's your bedroom, will it, Pryor? I can see what you're up to even if Beth's too naïve to catch on.'

Daniel looked at him as if he was something that had crawled out from under a log.

'Get out of my house,' he said in a low, deadly voice, 'before I drop you in your tracks.'

Warren strode to the door, his face contorted with rage. Then he turned and stabbed the air with his forefinger.

'All right, I'm going,' he spat. 'Back to LA. But she's coming with me. I'm not leaving her around here for the likes of you to get your filthy hands on. Come on, Beth, we're leaving!'

Beth stared at him in dismay.

'It's up to you, Beth,' warned Daniel. 'You're the one who'll have to decide whether I'm trying to take advantage of you.'

Beth's face flamed as she recalled that scene in the conservatory the previous evening. But honesty would not allow her to lay all the blame at Daniel's door. She had been willing. All too willing. And perhaps for that very reason it would be better for her to go. She hesitated with a tormented expression on her face. Without even realising it, she looked at Daniel for guidance.

'I'm not in the habit of seducing unwilling women,' said Daniel, replying to her unspoken question. 'If anything ever happens between us, it will have to be entirely of your own free will.'

'If anything ever happens!' spluttered Warren. 'You bastard! You're going to make damn sure that it does, aren't you? Don't you realise this girl is engaged to me?'

'Is she?' challenged Daniel sceptically.

Warren's eyes shifted away.

'I tell you this, Beth,' he muttered. 'I'm not standing for any more of this nonsense. Either you come back to LA with me right now or it's all over between us. Got it?'

Beth cast him an anguished look. 'But what about our clothing collection?' she cried.

'Stuff the clothing collection!' exclaimed Warren. 'If you really cared about me, you'd put me before the clothing collection any time.'

'Don't let him paint you into a corner, Beth,' warned Daniel. 'He's only trying to manipulate you. You don't have to give in. It's your choice.'

Warren shot Daniel a glance filled with hatred and then crossed the room to Beth. Seizing her by both arms, he shook her angrily.

'For the last time,' he insisted, 'are you coming with me or not?'

Beth hesitated.

'I can't, Warren!' she protested. 'It's not only my hopes that are riding on this project. Other people are involved too. My mother gave me a thousand dollars towards my air fare, which she really couldn't afford. You know she couldn't! And so long as there's any chance of replacing this collection, I've got to keep trying. I can't just let her down. Don't you see?'

Warren ignored her pleading expression.

'I don't think your mother is half as hard up as she likes to pretend,' he snorted. 'Anyway, I think you're wasting your time and I'm certainly not getting dragged into all this extra work for nothing. I'm going back to LA. Now are you coming with me or not?'

A sudden wave of rebellion rose in Beth's heart. Her eyes met Daniel's and she looked away hastily.

'No,' she muttered.

Warren swore violently under his breath and made for the door again.

'I will see you in LA at the show, won't I?' demanded Beth, hurrying after him.

'Don't count on it,' snapped Warren and he slammed the door behind him.

Beth sank down on to the sofa and covered her face with her hands.

'Good for you,' said Daniel approvingly, gripping her shoulder.

She shrugged off his hand with an impatient movement.

'Oh, I hope I did the right thing,' she fretted. 'It makes me feel so guilty to see Warren leaving like that.'

'So you're going to fall to pieces about it, are you?'

The taunt was as sharp and sudden as a slap in the face. Beth's head jerked up and her hands moved back into her lap, curling instinctively into fists of rage. A moment before she had felt like bursting into tears, but now she felt like hitting someone.

'How dare you?' she cried. 'It's all your fault. If you hadn't goaded him like that, he wouldn't have left!'

'Don't worry, sweetheart,' retorted Daniel. 'If you ask me, having him go forever is the best thing that could possibly happen to you.'

'He hasn't gone forever!' flashed Beth. 'He'll come back; he always does.'

Daniel sat down on a chair and leaned forward with his powerful forearms on his muscular thighs. 'Oh, so he makes a habit of this, does he?' he challenged. 'Throwing *prima donna* tantrums and walking out on you?'

'Don't be so hateful!' blazed Beth. 'If I weren't a guest in your house and if I weren't under an obligation to you about these clothes, I'd——'

'You'd what?' purred Daniel. 'You'd lash out at me like the stormy little spitfire I've always sensed you are, instead of the porcelain doll you pretend to be? Well, go ahead, tell me what you really think of me. I'd like to know. Although I can't expect any shrewd insights from a girl who wants to marry a man like that.'

Beth gulped for breath.

'All right, you asked for it,' she seethed. 'If you want to know the truth, I think you're arrogant, ruthless and manipulative! You ride over people like a steamroller and you don't give them a chance to make any choices of their own. And you're totally unscrupulous about the way you use your assets to convince them to do what you want. Just because you're loaded with power and money and sex appeal——'

'With what?' asked Daniel pleasantly.

Beth winced and felt a fiery colour mount to her cheeks. 'Sex appeal,' she stammered faintly.

Daniel stroked his chin and a glint came into his dark eyes.

'Yes, I thought that was what you said,' he murmured smugly. 'But don't let me interrupt. Continue.'

Beth flashed him a murderous look.

'You're hateful,' she cried unsteadily. 'You know perfectly well what I mean. There's some kind of extraordinary magnetism which you use to browbeat people even when they're really unwilling to do what you want.'

Daniel's whole body tensed so that he looked like a hunting panther about to strike.

'Unwilling?' he growled. 'Are you telling me you were unwilling in the conservatory last night?'

Beth hung her head.

'Yes,' she cried. And then honesty overwhelmed her. 'No... I don't know! You make me so confused I don't know anything any more and I hate it. I don't feel as if I'm in control of my life. It makes me so angry.'

'I see,' agreed Daniel, nodding thoughtfully. 'Angry. And you're quite sure it's me you're angry with?'

'What do you mean?' demanded Beth defensively. 'Who else could it be?'

Daniel smiled sardonically.

'Yourself,' he suggested. 'Or that fool that you're involved with.'

'Leave Warren out of this!' Beth flared. 'What I feel towards you is nothing to do with him.'

'Isn't it?' he challenged. 'Are you sure that you aren't angry with him for abandoning you for twenty-four hours without even trying to find out how you were? Or for refusing to buck in and help you do a difficult job? Or that you aren't angry with yourself for resenting him and feeling attracted to me?'

Beth clapped her hands over her ears. 'Stop it!' she begged.

Daniel grabbed her hands and hauled them away. 'The truth hurts, doesn't it?' he taunted.

'It isn't the truth!'

'Isn't it?' His eyes were dark with tiny, glimmering points of light at the centre of the pupils and his face was thrust so close to hers that she could see the predatory curve of his nose, the dark shadow of his beard beneath his skin and smell the faint, spicy aroma of his aftershave mingled with the powerful, arousing scent of his body. She let out breath in a long, harsh sigh.

'No,' she gasped.

This time his smile was no more than a bitter sneer.

'You're lying,' he growled.

'No, I'm not!' protested Beth, trying to step backwards out of his hold. But he drew her relentlessly towards him, pressing her so close against him that she could feel the heat of his body through the thin clothes and sense the tension in his muscles. Every nerve in her body quivered at that contact and for an instant she swayed against him, letting her eyes flutter closed as she surrendered to the spell of his vibrant masculinity. Then the image of Warren flashed into her mind and she froze like a statue in his arms. Suddenly she was conscious only of the agonised need to escape.

'No!' she cried through clenched teeth. 'Let me go, damn you! I've got work to do. It's nearly eleven o'clock.'

He released her and stepped back a pace but his eyes continued to hold her ensnared, as pitiless as search lights trained on a quivering animal.

'All right,' he agreed in a tone that was soft with menace. 'You do have work to do, so we won't discuss it now.'

Beth fled back to the ballroom in a state of turmoil. Yet fortunately she had always had the gift of being able

to lose herself in her work and she was reasonably sure
that nobody noticed her dismay. She continued working
steadily until seven p.m. when the second shift of dressmakers came on duty. By then she was exhausted and
ready to join the others in the main dining-room for an
excellent dinner served by Benson. To her relief Daniel
did not appear at the meal. And when it was over she
went back to her room, took a long, luxurious spa bath
and fell into bed. The next day followed the same pattern
of frantic activity until seven minutes after four o'clock
in the afternoon, when Wendy let out a riotous shriek.

'Whoop, whoop, woo! We've finished, girls! That is
absolutely, positively the last stitch.'

Uproar broke out and the stamping and cheering and
clapping brought Benson and Daniel running from the
other end of the house. Beth flinched when she saw
Daniel enter the room. But the lurking smile in his eyes
and around the corners of his lips gave no hint that there
had been any quarrel with her.

'Does this mean what I hope it does?' he queried.

'Yes, sir!' cried Wendy. 'Signed, sealed and delivered,
one autumn collection of clothing, finished and ready
to go.'

Daniel marched down the centre of the ballroom like
a triumphant general, shook Wendy's hand, kissed her
on both cheeks and then turned to Beth. Smiling sardonically, he kissed her on both cheeks too, then turned
away.

'Well done, everyone!' he said. 'Benson, I think this
calls for champagne.'

Amid the pop of corks, the bubbling of golden yellow
liquid and the laughter and exhausted groans of the
workers, Beth found herself feeling suddenly as shy and
awkward as a teenager. She could not be unaware of the
way Daniel's eyes followed her around the room. And

when he came across to her with a smoking green bottle and a couple of long-stemmed crystal glasses clutched in his other hand, she dropped her eyes and felt herself flush. Setting down the glasses on a handy sewing-table, he poured them both a generous measure of the fizzy gold liquid.

'Well, here's to my beautiful bride of Santa Barbara,' he said in the deep, vibrant voice that made her skin prickle.

She took a hasty sip of the champagne and swallowed hard, gasping as the bubbles seemed to explode inside her head. A light, airy dizziness swam through her veins.

'I owe it all to you,' she admitted reluctantly. 'I would never in a million years have thought of doing this.'

'It's nice to know I'm appreciated.'

Was she mistaken or did she detect a hint of sarcasm in that? But before she had time to decide, Daniel continued on.

'Well, there's no point standing around here wasting time. Now that the clothes are finished, I don't want to leave anything else to chance. So as soon as you've had your champagne, get changed and we'll leave for Los Angeles immediately. Wendy and the girls can pack up the collection for you in tissue paper.'

Beth stared at him, feeling slightly stunned. 'You want to go to Los Angeles tonight?' she echoed.

'That's right. The show is tomorrow and we can't take any chances of being late. The traffic on the freeways in the morning can be something fierce.'

'But where can I stay?' she demanded. 'I still don't have any money. My handbag went down with the motor launch and I haven't had time to go near a bank. I'll have to——'

But Daniel cut her off with an exasperated gesture. 'You'll stay with me. I have an apartment in Los Angeles.'

Beth was too stunned to protest, with the result that half an hour later she found herself in the Jaguar with Daniel, heading south along the coast road. The sun was already low in the sky and the air was filled with an incredible haze of colour, wild rose, gold and pale lavender. Far out to sea the stark, black shapes of the oil-rigs loomed like science fiction monsters appearing from the deep, while ahead of them the dark, oncoming crags of the coastline plummeted sharply into the sea. Beth was filled with a confused mixture of emotions. Exhaustion, resentment, apprehension and an incredulous, radiant happiness that bubbled through her as if the champagne were still at work.

'Did you know that this road follows the track of the old Spanish explorers?' asked Daniel. '"*El Camino Real*", they used to call it. The Royal Road.'

'Really?' echoed Beth. 'How fascinating! What were they doing here?'

Daniel's smile held a hint of bitterness. 'The same as the rest of us who flocked to California,' he replied. 'Looking for adventure, or gold, or both. Every time I drive this way I think of them riding along on their horses with their wide sombreros on their heads and their silver spurs jingling. And this whole wonderful country like an untamed paradise opening up in front of them.'

Beth sighed appreciatively.

'Yes, I suppose they were pretty romantic figures,' she agreed.

'Well, I wouldn't glamorise them too much,' warned Daniel. 'They may have been out there pursuing their dreams, but dreams aren't always noble. Some of them were probably men with genuine vision who wanted to leave the place better than they found it, but others just wanted to exploit the land and the people and to hell with the consequences.'

I wonder which group you would have come into, thought Beth silently. A strange, wistful thrill ran through her body at the picture that conjured up. She imagined Daniel dressed in a white ruffled shirt, black trousers, sombrero and ornate riding boots, mounted on a black stallion and riding along this magnificent road that dipped and swooped over every headland. He would make a very commanding figure on horseback, she thought, although he was far taller than any Spanish explorer was likely to have been. But there was something about the visionary gleam in his dark eyes, the assertive thrust of his chin that made her feel that he would have endured any hardship to the bitter end in order to conquer the country he had staked out for himself. And what would he have done then? she wondered. Would he have fallen in love and built a hacienda for the woman of his choice? Disturbed at the trend her thoughts were taking, she wound down the window and inhaled a deep breath of the fresh, salt air. By now it was taking on the chill of evening and it was as cold and crisp as a draught of white wine laced with a subtle bouquet of flowers.

'Well, I suppose a lot of people have travelled along this road pursuing their dreams,' she said pensively.

'And you're one of them,' replied Daniel. 'You've worked like a demon getting this collection together and by tomorrow night you and I are going to be celebrating.'

Something about that phrase 'you and I' pierced Beth to the heart. It suggested something far more intimate than the turbulent and rather odd business relationship that she and Daniel had formed in the last few days. And the brooding sideways glance that he flashed her only reinforced her misgivings. She felt the same terror and elation that she might have experienced standing on the edge of a high cliff and wondering whether she was about to fall or soar. But that question was more than she wanted to deal with at the moment, so she simply flashed him a small, tight smile.

'I'm rather tired,' she said in a subdued voice. 'I think I might take a rest, if you don't mind?'

His mouth tightened but he did not argue with her.

'Sure, go ahead,' he agreed. 'I want you looking your best at the parade tomorrow.'

Closing her eyes, Beth hunched back into the luxurious leather seat. But, in spite of her exhaustion she found it difficult to unwind enough to go to sleep. With an effort she forced herself to breathe in a deep, regular rhythm that would discourage Daniel from conversation. But she found herself running over and over the same thoughts like a jogger on a treadmill. The quarrel with Warren, the way Daniel had kissed her in the conservatory, their puzzling, tempestuous business relationship, the parade tomorrow. And, try as she might, she could not simply let go and drift. A faint click reached her ears, the sounds of buttons being pressed and then Daniel's hoarse, velvety voice.

'Try this,' he suggested in amusement. 'It might stop you worrying and let you doze off.'

The soothing notes of a Chopin Polonaise leapt into the air as pure and sweet as crystal. Beneath the music Beth heard the whizz of a passing car, the hiss of their own tyres on the road and felt her tense muscles slowly begin to relax. Her last thought as she drifted off was, How on earth did Daniel know I was still awake and worrying? Can he read my mind?

Her sleep was serene and refreshing and when she finally woke it was like coming up to the surface from a deep, cool pool of water. She turned her head and found Daniel's hand resting on her shoulder. All around them was darkness except for the bright lights that sparkled like brilliantly coloured necklaces against the velvety blackness.

'Where are we?' she asked, yawning and blinking.

'Los Angeles,' replied Daniel. 'Welcome to the city of dreams.'

CHAPTER FOUR

THE muted hum of conversation vibrated up to meet Beth as she peered over the edge of the upstairs gallery in Cadogan Hall the following morning. Only ten more minutes till noon and still no sign of Warren in the audience below. Five designers' collections had already been displayed and, at the very least, he should have come to view those. After all, wasn't that part of his job? Part of what his parents paid him for? Instead he had chosen to stay away from the entire show, just to show his annoyance with Beth. Well, damn him! she thought. A sick feeling of misery, nerves and anger surged up inside her, but she paid no attention. Her feelings didn't matter. What mattered was getting this show on the road and not disappointing the team who had helped her. She caught a glimpse of a dark glossy head, which could only be Daniel's. A pang of some indefinable emotion shot through Beth's body. She wasn't even sure that she liked Daniel, but she certainly owed him a lot. And, however bitterly they might have quarrelled, he was here when she needed him most. But where on earth was Warren?

A husky voice broke in on her reverie.

'Beth? You want to come check that we're all dressed right?'

It was Laura Mae Harper, a black model from Georgia with the regal dignity of an African queen. As they made their way back to the dressing-rooms, she squeezed Beth's arm comfortingly.

'Hey, don't look so gloomy, honey! Your designs are great. They're gonna be a smash hit!'

'Do you really think so?' asked Beth miserably.

'Just watch it happen!' urged Laura Mae.

But it wasn't until the show was nearly over that Beth was finally convinced. Peeping out from the wings behind the catwalk, she saw Laura Mae swirling around in the wedding-dress against a halo of bright, natural light. And suddenly the catchy music from the loud-speakers was drowned by a growing thunder of applause. Holding her breath, Beth tiptoed away until she was safely inside a deserted dressing-room. Then she jumped into the air and let out a stifled whoop of excitement. She was so thrilled that she wanted to share this moment with everyone, even Warren. But it wasn't Warren who came backstage to congratulate her ten minutes later. It was Daniel.

'Well, are you feeling proud?' he asked. 'You ought to be.'

Beth pulled a face at him. Some of the euphoria had already worn off and she was beginning to worry that the applause was mere courtesy.

'Do you really think it was a success?' she asked anxiously.

'It was dynamite,' insisted Daniel. 'You're going to find yourself a very busy and very wealthy woman before too much longer. Now that you're over the first hurdle, you'd better get ready for the second one. It's crucial for you to shine at this lunch too. The social side of doing business is important anywhere, but it's vital in Los Angeles.'

Beth heaved a sigh.

'I hate that sort of thing,' she said. 'I've always been shy and I'm just not good at it. Besides, I've no idea where Warren has got to. I looked everywhere for him before the parade ended, but I couldn't find him.'

'Never mind about Warren,' snapped Daniel impatiently. 'You can sort out your personal problems any time. But there are moments when your work has to come first and this is one of them. Agreed?'

'I suppose so,' muttered Beth.

'Good. Well, come on.'

Five minutes later a silently gliding lift disgorged them on to a rooftop terrace on the fifth floor of the building. Beth stopped dead in amazement at the sight that met her eyes. The terrace must have been eighty feet long and nearly as wide, but the entire perimeter of it had been enclosed in screens of white silk. Against this background were tubs containing orange and lemon trees, their foliage green and glossy against the pale background. Smaller terracotta urns were bright with cascades of red geraniums and blue lobelias and in the centre of the terrace a string quartet of musicians dressed in white clothes were playing a Vivaldi sonata. Arranged in a circle around the central plaza were round tables with shady white umbrellas, but nobody was sitting at these yet. Instead a huge crowd of people was milling around on the red-brick paving, laughing and chattering and uttering shrill squeals of excitement. Somewhere a champagne cork popped loudly and Beth heard the chime of crystal glasses and the clatter of silver. She hesitated, feeling decidedly intimidated by the hum of noisy conversation, the white glare of photographers' flashes and the glimpse of several internationally famous celebrities.

'What do we do now?' she whispered, unconsciously shrinking closer to Daniel.

'Stop acting like a clinging vine for a start,' replied Daniel under his breath. Adroitly he shrugged her off, so that a good two feet of brick paving lay between them. 'You don't need me for support, do you?'

It was brutal, but effective. For a split second Beth stared at him with a look of frozen shock and dismay on her face. Then her chin came up, her shoulders squared and her eyes flashed blue fire.

'No, I certainly don't!' she hissed angrily. 'In fact, why don't you just take yourself off? I can manage perfectly well without you.'

Daniel smiled lazily.

'Oh, there's no need for that,' he murmured. 'You forget that we have business interests in common. So we'll circulate fashionably together. But just remember that I don't want you all over me like a rash.'

Beth felt her shyness being shrivelled up by a fierce, scorching anger.

'I wish I *were* all over you like a rash!' she muttered. 'Smallpox, for preference!'

But Daniel seemed indifferent to her sarcasm.

'Come on,' he urged, plunging into the crowd. 'Let's get something to eat and then we'll circulate.'

Beth followed him sulkily, feeling as if she could plunge a knife into the back of his smart beige summer suit. Her first instinctive reaction to Daniel Pryor had been one of wary mistrust, but a lot had happened in the few days since the boating accident. And, in spite of their quarrel about Warren she had found herself increasingly drawn to Daniel. Besides, he hadn't seemed entirely indifferent to her. So why was he behaving like this now? Just when she was beginning to trust him and feel grateful to him, he was slamming the door in her face. It made her feel hurt and puzzled. And very, very annoyed.

The buffet was arranged at the far end of the terrace with a squadron of black-uniformed waiters around it.

Following Daniel's example, Beth picked up a Wedgwood plate and chose some succulent king prawns with a dipping sauce of Tabasco and thousand island dressing, a small square of hot savoury cheese in filo pastry and a few cherry tomatoes.

'Champagne?' asked Daniel.

Beth shook her head.

'I'll just have an orange juice, please,' she replied coldly.

She had thought she was too nervous to eat, but the food was delicious and the orange juice was freshly squeezed and clinking with cubes of ice. As they stood juggling plates and glasses, Daniel casually roped in a couple of guests who wandered by and introduced them to Beth. For a moment her usual shyness threatened to paralyse her, but then the memory of Daniel's cutting remark flashed back. Fighting down her urge to shrink and stammer, she forced herself to smile and chat intelligently. Before long she found herself at the centre of a friendly, laughing group and she began to relax a little. Deftly Daniel took her empty plate and glass and set them on a nearby table.

'Well, if you'll excuse us, we're going to mingle,' he said.

And mingle they did. Within the next fifteen minutes Beth found herself introduced to half a dozen buyers from both east- and west-coast stores, five film stars and several agents. By the time they sat down at a shady table to eat their main course she was rather enjoying herself. Conscious of Daniel's mocking gaze as they did their rounds, she had dredged up a courage that astonished her. It might be pure bravado, but she had waded in and tackled buyers with charm and determination. Now she had several important new contracts under her belt and a glowing sense of confidence to go with them.

As a waiter set a plate of sizzling charcoal-grill beef steak
in front of her accompanied by a gigantic jacket potato
lavishly filled with sour cream and chives and a plate of
green salad, she shot Daniel a look of triumph.

'Well,' she said challengingly. 'Are you convinced? I'm
not such a hopeless wimp after all, am I?'

His dark eyes held hers with a look that baffled her.
Was it amusement, contempt or something else?

'Oh, I suppose you're doing all right for a beginner,'
he replied, in dampening tones. 'But the day's not over
yet.'

The lack of enthusiasm in his voice made Beth
smoulder inwardly. She felt a simmering indignation
bubble up inside her and, along with it, a fierce determination to make Daniel sit up and take notice. However
hard she had to work, she wouldn't leave until she had
enough orders to pay him back twice over for the money
he had spent. That would show him!

The main course was followed by a luscious array of
desserts, but Beth waved away the hazelnut gateau and
strawberry shortcake in favour of a small bowl of tropical
fruit. Once the fragrant black coffee and chocolate
truffles appeared, people began to circulate again,
moving casually from table to table to chat with friends
or business acquaintances. Beth was just about rise to
her feet and join the fray when she heard a husky laugh
behind her. Swinging around with an enquiring look,
she saw that a deeply tanned brunette with a voluptuous
figure, curly black hair and huge brown eyes had just
materialised in the narrow gap between her chair and
Daniel's. The newcomer was only about five feet two
inches tall and her red and white dress was obviously
very expensive. Before Beth had the chance to notice
anything else, the brunette slung one arm around
Daniel's shoulders and leaned forward, enfolding him

in a cloud of perfume and a generous display of warm cleavage. Beth felt a stab of anger so sharp that it startled her. After all, what did it matter to her if some centre-fold pin-up girl chose to drape herself all over Daniel? She didn't care. Did she?

'Well, hi, Daniel,' cooed the brunette rapturously. 'Now don't say I never do anything for you. I turned up to the show just the way you asked!'

Just the way you asked . . . So Daniel had invited this purring sex kitten to the show, had he? No wonder he hadn't wanted Beth hanging around him! A shock of resentment seared through her as Daniel's gaze flickered lazily from her to the brunette. He's comparing us! thought Beth indignantly. How dare he? I suppose he's working out which one gives the best kisses! She felt even more indignant when she realised that Daniel's eyes were lingering on the other woman with unabashed admiration.

'Sunny, I'd like you to meet Beth Saxon,' said Daniel. 'Beth's a fashion designer just getting established. And this is Sunny Martino. She's one of our finest Hollywood actresses.'

Sunny wriggled joyously at the compliment.

'Well, thank you, sir,' she cried, laying one hand on Daniel's shoulder and batting her enormous eyelashes seductively. Then she gave a little shriek of laughter.

Beth's mouth tightened disapprovingly. Feather-brained idiot! she thought. And then Sunny's melting brown eyes skimmed from her to Daniel with a shrewd, speculative look that was anything but featherbrained. For a moment she wondered whether she was under-estimating the actress. Then Sunny pouted provocatively.

'Don't you have a place for me to sit down?' she complained.

'Let me get you a chair, Sunny,' offered Daniel.

He pulled out a chair for Sunny and moved along one space himself so that the actress was now seated between him and Beth. Sunny smiled mechanically at Beth and then leaned across at Daniel.

'Honey, I've been wanting to talk to you,' she murmured huskily. 'I've got a big problem with AYZ Studios and I need your advice. You see, my contract——'

At that moment there was an interruption as three photographers who had spotted Sunny appeared on the opposite side of the table and flashbulbs blazed rapidly. With only the faintest of sighs, Sunny lounged back into her chair, thrusting forward the magnificent cleavage and smiled winningly. A reporter appeared beside them, whipped out a notebook and pencil and began asking Sunny some questions. She was still babbling engagingly when another figure hovered into sight.

'Warren!' exclaimed Beth. 'So you came! Did you see the collection?'

Over the past few days she had been feelingly increasingly annoyed with Warren for leaving her in the lurch in Santa Barbara, but now her resentment was tempered with relief. The worry that Warren might have left permanently had been haunting her and, in some obscure way, she felt that his presence would protect her against Daniel. And, with Daniel making eyes at Sunny Martino, it gave Beth's pride a boost to have another male come in search of her. Particularly one as good-looking as Warren. Ushering him into a seat, she flashed him a welcoming smile and was gratified to see Daniel scowl.

'Hi, Beth,' said Warren, sitting down at the table with nothing in his manner to suggest that they had ever quarrelled. 'Sure, I saw it. We did a pretty good job, didn't we?'

'Yes, didn't we?' agreed Beth rather coolly. She might be pleased to see Warren, but that was going just a little too far. How like him to want to claim the credit when he hadn't done any of the work!

The reporter paused with his pencil in mid-air, sensing a story.

'Hey, are you guys the people behind Warbeth designs?' he asked. 'The collection that was such a smash hit today?'

'That's right,' agreed Warren.

The reporter darted a quick look at Sunny.

'Well, look, can you stick around?' he asked. 'Maybe when Miss Martino and I have finished——'

Sunny dissolved into giggles.

'Oh, we've finished now!' she cried and blew the reporter a kiss. 'I know you'll say all the right things about me. So go ahead and interview these people while Daniel and I have our coffee.'

But the interview wasn't a complete success. For one thing, Beth was irrationally annoyed by Sunny's apparent inability to spoon sugar or stir coffee without help from Daniel. And, for another, Warren simply elbowed her out of the discussion. He had always had the kind of personality that loved the limelight and he was quick to jump in and field the reporter's questions before Beth had a chance to answer. Before long her relief at his return gave way to a growing irritation. She resented the way he took credit for most of the designs and for all of the business side of putting the collection together. He also kept turning the conversation round to the subject of his parents' chain of clothing stores in Australia. But the most distressing moment of all for Beth came when one of the reporters asked a completely routine question.

'So did you have any problems getting your designs here safely from Australia?' he asked.

Warren laughed boyishly.

'No, we didn't have any trouble on the way here!' he exclaimed. 'But we certainly did have some trouble in Santa Barbara. We were taking some fashion photos on a launch on the harbour when——'

Indignation and dismay rose in Beth. Without even knowing why, she felt passionately certain that she did not want the details of the accident and its aftermath splashed all over the newspapers for other people to gape at.

'—when we had a rather unpleasant accident,' finished Warren dramatically.

'That sounds interesting,' said one of the reporters. 'Would you like to tell us about it?'

'Sure,' began Warren.

But he was foiled by Daniel's lazy interruption.

'Say, have you guys heard that I'm thinking of making a new series of *Destiny's Favourite*?' he asked. 'Naturally it'll be starring Sunny Martino and some other big-name actors.'

Beth and Warren were instantly forgotten amid a hubbub of excitement and the cameras began to flash again. Daniel and Sunny obligingly cuddled close together and flashed radiant smiles which made Beth suffer an obscure pang of annoyance. Warren began talking about the accident in Santa Barbara again, trying to arouse the reporters' interest, but Daniel adroitly headed him off.

'I'm also thinking of inviting Lane Galloway to play the male lead,' he said. 'I see he's right over there at that other table. Maybe you guys would like to come and get a picture of us all together.'

In a moment the table was abandoned in a hectic rush and Warren and Beth found themselves alone.

'Pryor is such a ratbag,' complained Warren. 'What a publicity-hunter! Did you see how he had to turn the reporters' attention on himself immediately? He couldn't bear to see us in the limelight for one minute, could he?'

Beth pulled a face. 'I'm glad he couldn't,' she said with feeling. 'I really didn't want to talk about how it felt to be half drowned or to walk through the Yacht Club in a borrowed bathrobe. Personally I'd rather keep my private life private.'

Warren sighed impatiently. 'What's so private about it?' he demanded. 'It would have been great publicity for the collection. And with the way things are beginning to take off, I think we should take advantage of every bit of help we can get.'

'We?' prompted Beth with renewed grievance. 'I thought you didn't want any more to do with it. You walked out rather than help to replace the collection, remember!'

Warren reddened. His tanned, neatly manicured hands crept across the table and seized hers.

'I'm sorry, Beth,' he said coaxingly. 'I was just so jealous when I found you staying with that creep. I couldn't think straight. But I want you to know that from here on I'm with you all the way. It's a full partnership as of now.'

'Is it?' asked Beth bitterly. 'And what exactly does that mean?'

Warren's eyes widened in surprise.

'Why, probably that we form some kind of company,' he said. 'The way things are going now I think we're going to be a big hit as designers, you and I.'

Beth withdrew her hand from his grip and pressed her lips together to stop them quivering.

'I see,' she replied evenly. 'A business partnership. And what about the rest of our lives, Warren? What other kind of partnership did you have in mind?'

Warren's voice was suddenly warm, caressing.

'We'll go back to the way we were before,' he murmured. 'Silly Beth, did you really think I'd left you forever? There's no need to look so tragic, darling, nothing is going to change between us.'

'That's exactly what I'm afraid of,' snapped Beth. 'Nothing ever does change, does it? You're bright and cheerful during the good times, Warren, but, when the bad times hit, you don't want to know me, do you? You just leave me to cope with it all on my own!'

Warren stared at her in consternation. 'Beth,' he said in a reproving undertone. 'People are looking at you.'

She glanced around and saw that a couple of heads were turned in their direction. Embarrassment flooded through her and she rose to her feet. Coming hot on the heels of Daniel's little tête-à-tête with Sunny, Warren's calm assumption that nothing had changed between them was more than she could bear. Were all men nothing but selfish egotists? Did Daniel really think he could kiss her passionately one minute and waltz off with a glamorous actress the next? And did Warren honestly believe he could abandon her in a crisis and then come back a few days later as if nothing had happened? Beth had always thought of herself as calm, serious, reserved, but she was shocked by a sudden impulse to shout and weep and throw things. With a determined effort she regained control of herself.

'You're right,' she admitted unsteadily. 'We can't talk about it here. And anyway, I'm too upset at the moment. Why don't you phone me at Daniel's apartment? It's listed in the telephone directory.'

And with that she turned and plunged blindly into the crowd. She had no clear idea of where she was going, but before she had advanced twelve paces she blundered straight into Daniel, who was standing with his arm around Sunny. He took one look at her troubled face and released his hold on Sunny.

'Can we take a raincheck on this conversation?' he asked the actress. 'It's time Beth and I were getting out of here.'

'Sure,' agreed Sunny. Once again her brown eyes met Beth's with a challenging, speculative expression. Then she gave a faint, twisted smile. 'Take my advice, honey, and be very careful what you do from here on. There are a lot of wolves in this town and they don't hesitate to gobble up babes in the wood. I'd hate to see you get hurt.'

Beth gave her a startled glance and murmured some inaudible reply. What on earth did Sunny mean? Was she warning Beth off Daniel? If so, she needn't bother, thought Beth sourly. After getting the brush-off today, I'm hardly likely to go chasing after him. Not that I ever was! And Warren is just as bad. She didn't ask herself why Daniel's flirtation with Sunny should cause her so much more pain and anger than Warren's clumsy attempt to gloss over their quarrel. All she felt was a childlike urge to bolt and run for cover.

Somehow she managed to keep her head high and a smile on her face as Daniel shepherded her though the crowd to the edge of the terrace. But once they were safely inside the lift she gave up all pretence of control. Closing her eyes, she leaned her head against its wall and fought back tears.

'Warren?' asked Daniel.

She nodded wordlessly. It was easier and less humiliating to agree than to try and explain her complicated feeling about Sunny.

'That bastard,' said Daniel softly. 'Here, take this.' He handed her a clean white handkerchief. 'No tears until we're safely out of this place. There may still be photographers down on the sidewalk and I want you smiling when you walk past them. Got it?'

Beth opened her eyes and took a long, shuddering breath.

'Got it,' she agreed.

But her lips twisted bitterly as she scrubbed her face with Daniel's handkerchief. How easy and convenient for Daniel to assume that Warren was the sole cause of her distress! As if his own behaviour in kissing her passionately and then falling all over some actress didn't matter a damn. Well, it probably didn't to him, she reflected grimly. Men were all the same, especially men with smouldering animal magnetism. Untrustworthy and interested in only one thing. But he's not getting it from me, thought Beth, so he'd better not try again! By the time they reached Daniel's apartment her misery had subsided to a hollow ache in the pit of her stomach. When Daniel opened the door into the marble-floored entrance hall, with its huge gilt mirrors and claw-footed antique tables, she felt a rush of relief almost as if she were coming home. After the tension of the day the apartment seemed like a welcome refuge. And, although Beth had an ominous feeling that there was a confrontation brewing, she was content to postpone it as long as possible.

'Go and sit in the living-room and take it easy while I fix you a drink,' Daniel ordered.

Obediently she slogged into the living-room, kicked off her shoes and flopped on to a deep cream leather couch. Two minutes later Daniel appeared beside her, hauled her into a sitting position and thrust a large gin and tonic into her hand. She took a sip of the chilled, bitter drink and shuddered.

'Right,' said Daniel as briskly as if he were chairing a meeting. 'The first thing you need to do is get rid of that goddamned Warren. So why don't you call him up right now and tell him it's all over?'

Beth choked on her drink. The arrogance of this suggestion took her breath away and it was several moments before she could speak.

'Why? To clear the way for you?' she flared.

Daniel shrugged indifferently.

'It would certainly make things easier for our relationship.'

There was a tense silence, broken only by Beth's incredulous gasp for air.

'I don't believe I'm hearing this!' she spluttered. 'What relationship? The one you're hoping to have with me when Sunny Martino is too busy to oblige you?'

A twisted smile played around the corners of Daniel's mouth.

'So, it upset you to see me with Sunny, did it?'

'I didn't say that!'

'You didn't have to,' he growled, seizing her arm. 'It's written all over you!'

Beth's heart hammered wildly and she had to consciously resist the impulse to sink into Daniel's embrace. His hard brown fingers were gripping her arm and it would have been easy, so fatally easy to bring her right hand over to cover his. She could almost feel the warmth of his wrist, the coarse dark hair, the tension of muscle and sinew. But if she yielded to the urge to let her fingers flutter over his, to look up into his eyes, she would be lost. There would be no going back. Because she wanted Daniel Pryor as she had never wanted any man in her life. And if she touched him, or looked at him, he would guess the truth. Dropping her gaze, she broke away from him in panic. 'I'm just telling you that I'm not prepared to be some kind of sex object for you. Good enough to kiss in private, but not fit to be acknowledged in public! I was just a little interlude before you got back to your real interest, Sunny Martino, wasn't I? You didn't even want to know me at that lunch today!'

'Don't be a fool!' snarled Daniel. 'That place was crawling with reporters, which was why I trod very carefully. I knew you wouldn't want a lot of imaginative smut about your relationship with me splashed over the tabloids tomorrow.'

'Whereas Sunny would?' taunted Beth.

Daniel shrugged.

'Sunny and I have been lovers for the last seven years,' he said indifferently.

Beth felt a pang as sharp and hurtful as if she had been stabbed. She caught her breath.

'Or so the tabloids say,' finished Daniel, eyeing her from under half-closed lids.

She felt her fingernails dig deep into her palms. 'Is it true?' she asked hoarsely.

'What would it matter to you?' countered Daniel. 'You're not interested in getting involved with me. Are you?'

'No!' she insisted violently. 'Obviously all you want is sex and as much variety as possible in your partners. Well, I'm not interested in that kind of relationship, thanks very much.'

'What kind of relationship are you interested in?'

'One with commitment,' retorted Beth, tossing her head. 'One where both partners genuinely care about each other and are loyal through thick and thin.'

'I see,' Daniel murmured in velvety tones. 'Like the one you have with Warren?'

Her head jerked back as if he had slapped her. Rage swept through her.

'That's not fair,' she whispered hoarsely.

'Isn't it?' taunted Daniel, his face so close to hers that she could see the blue-black shadow of his beard under his skin.

Her legs felt so weak that they would scarcely hold her. She opened her mouth to reply, but the words wouldn't come. She stared at Daniel in dismay, willing him to stop this torment.

And, before she could protest, he took her face in his hands and stared down at her with a ferocity and passion that electrified her. For a moment she gazed back at him, feeling her lips part and her body quiver in a frenzy of need as urgent as his own. Then she broke away, shuddering.

'No!' she cried despairingly.

He took a step backwards, his dark eyes blazing, his mouth a narrow, contemptuous line.

'All right,' he rasped. 'If that's your choice, get dressed and we'll go out for a farewell dinner.'

CHAPTER FIVE

' "FAREWELL"?' echoed Beth in consternation.

'Yes,' agreed Daniel with a shrug. 'After all, that's what you want, isn't it? The fashion show is over, so there's no real need for us to see each other ever again. Is there?'

Beth stared at him with a sudden acute sense of dismay. She felt devastated. Deep inside her there was a frozen sensation of pain and disbelief, along with a feeling of unfinished business. Of course she wasn't in love with Daniel, but she had somehow thought there would be more quarrels, plans, shared endeavours ahead of them. Now she felt almost cheated to discover that she was wrong.

'No, I suppose not,' she agreed bleakly.

Daniel smiled at her. His momentary anger seemed to have vanished and it was hard to believe that he had gazed at her so stormily only moments before.

'Well, then, a farewell dinner seems in order, doesn't it?' he continued. 'It's been a pleasant relationship, so it's only right to mark the end of it, wouldn't you say?'

Beth stared mutely back at him, hating him. Obviously he didn't feel any of the bittersweet torment that engulfed her at the thought of parting. But pride forced her to wear a false smile.

'Yes, of course,' she agreed, and was furious to hear a tremor in her voice.

'Good,' said Daniel briskly. 'Then I'll book a table at Emilio's.'

Some of Beth's tension slowly ebbed away. At least he hadn't noticed her agitation, she thought, watching him stride across to the table and pick up the phone. But, if he really cared about her, he would have noticed, wouldn't he? Well, she'd been a fool to think that his kisses meant anything, but all she could do now was try and salvage her pride. Go to this wretched dinner and show him that she could be just as casual and blasé as he was. And then part with him forever. The deceitful, smooth-talking beast!

'Right. Emilio's at eight o'clock,' announced Daniel, hanging up the receiver. 'I've got to go out on business now, but I'll be back at seven-thirty to pick you up.'

Left alone, Beth sank on to the sofa with a groan. She should have been enthralled at the success of the show, but instead she felt too drained to appreciate it. Anger, confusion and dismay threatened to overwhelm her and, in a muddled way, it all seemed to be centred on Daniel. Yet there was also the problem of her relationship with Warren to tackle and at the moment she felt quite unable to face it. Shaking her head, she decided to go and have a hot bath. If Warren phoned, she would simply have to talk to him and decide where the relationship was going, but she dreaded the encounter. Fortunately, even though she left her bathroom door open while she soaked in a tub of hot water, she did not hear the telephone ring. At last, dressed in a comfortable towelling tracksuit, she lay down on her bed and fell asleep.

It was just after seven o'clock when she was woken by a knock on her bedroom door. Sleepily she sat up.

'Warren?' she said.

The answer came back, infuriatingly cheerful.

'No, it's Daniel. Time to get dressed, sweetheart.'

Sweetheart, thought Beth indignantly. I'm not your sweetheart and I never will be. Yet she dressed carefully in one of the outfits from her collection. An attractive cocktail dress in a clinging blue chiffon woven with silver thread, a wide silver belt and matching silver shoes. Daniel said nothing when she emerged from her room, but his eyes roved over her body with an unmistakable spark of admiration. Beth felt a confused rush of pleasure and annoyance and tried not to look too closely at him. He was wearing a black dinner suit, immaculate white shirt and black tie and he exuded a smouldering aura of sensuality. Stay calm, she ordered herself frantically. Don't let him upset you. Just remember that this is Hollywood and you're just as sophisticated and glitzy as he is!

Emilio's proved to be a glamorous restaurant on Melrose Avenue. As they entered the downstairs dining-room, Beth heard the splash of running water and gazed in awe at a miniature Trevi Fountain bathed in coloured lights. All around them were marble columns, brick archways, stained-glass windows and gilt-framed oil paintings. But before she could linger very long admiring the décor a smiling waiter came to greet them and led them upstairs to the cedar-panelled balcony.

Once they were settled in the candlelit booth, the waiter whipped out his pad and pencil and looked questioningly at Daniel.

'A pre-dinner drink, sir?' he suggested.

Daniel glanced at Beth. 'I think some champagne would be in order. Do you agree?'

'Yes, please,' she said as casually as if she drank champagne every night of the week.

'A bottle of Veuve Clicquot,' added Daniel.

Within moments the waiter returned with an ornate silver ice-bucket and two long-stemmed glasses. There was a discreet pop, a trail of vapour and then when both glasses were filled the waiter withdrew, leaving them alone.

'Well,' said Daniel, raising his glass, 'here's to us!'

Beth looked at him doubtfully, her heart beginning to hammer. There was something uncomfortably intimate about the wording of that, particularly when they were sitting here in a secluded booth lit by the soft glow of candles. But it seemed ridiculous to protest. After all, she was sophisticated and worldly, wasn't she?

'All right,' she said huskily. 'To us.'

As always, the dry, fizzy taste of the champagne gave her a feeling of dizzy exhilaration. She felt her cheeks flushing as she set down the glass and wondered whether it was her imagination or whether Daniel really was looking at her with keen, scrutinising urgency. She wondered even more when he reached inside his dinner-jacket and pulled out a long manila envelope which he laid on the table. Twisting her head slightly, she saw that her own name was typed on the front of it.

'What's that?' she asked in bewilderment, reaching for it.

But he seized her outstretched fingers and set them down on the table.

'Later,' he warned. 'It's just a legal document I had my attorneys prepare about our business relationship.'

'Oh,' murmured Beth.

She felt confused, slightly hurt and yet very, very curious. No doubt it was just some document arranging for her to make formal repayment of all the expenses of getting her fashion collection ready on time. If Daniel never intended to see her again after tonight, he would certainly want to know that his investment was safe. But she couldn't help feeling slightly aggrieved that he needed

to make sure of her in this way. Couldn't he have just
trusted her to pay him back?

'I did intend to pay you back as soon as I possibly
could,' she said rather stiffly.

His dark eyes glinted.

'I'm sure you did,' he purred. 'But, if I can have you
legally tied down by the terms agreed to in that
document, I'd feel much happier about our whole relationship. Now, would you like to order some food?'

Beth flashed him a stormy look but accepted the
leather-covered menu and stared down at it sightlessly.
The words 'farewell dinner' kept ringing in her head and
it was two or three minutes before her tempestuous
feelings calmed enough to let her concentrate. Even then
she found herself frowning in perplexity over the unfamiliar items.

'I'll have the stru—stra—the chicken and egg soup,'
she said. 'And then the veal dish with the fried potatoes
and salad. I can't say it, the one with lemon.'

Daniel's lips twitched.

'*Piccata al limone*,' he replied. 'A good choice.'

While they waited for the food to arrive, they chatted
about the fashion show earlier in the day and the rooftop
lunch, but Beth did not mention the two people who
were most on her mind from that lunchtime meeting:
Warren and Sunny. And neither did Daniel. Only when
the last delicious mouthful of chicken soup had been
swallowed did the conversation become more personal,
and even then it took an unexpected turn.

'Were your parents happily married?' asked Daniel
abruptly.

Beth stared at him with a startled expression.

'What on earth does that have to do with anything?'
she demanded.

'More than you might think,' said Daniel cryptically. 'Come on, tell me. Were they?'

Beth frowned, casting her mind back to the small terraced house on the Rocks at Woolloomooloo where she had spent her childhood. A vivid rush of memory brought back her father's angry, querulous voice as her mother came in exhausted from the factory and began preparing tea. She sighed.

'I don't know,' she said. 'In a way I suppose they were. They stayed married for thirty-three years until he died two years ago.'

'That doesn't necessarily mean anything,' retorted Daniel. 'It might just mean that they had no choice. Nowhere else to go. But how did they act towards each other? Were they warm, affectionate, appreciative?'

Beth coiled one of her curls restlessly around her index finger and then let it go.

'No,' she admitted. 'My father was rather horrible to my mother, actually. From what my older sister says, he was always pretty short-tempered. The kind of man who loses his temper over nothing. And after the accident he complained all the time. Even though he was in a wheelchair, there were a lot of things that he could have done, but he wouldn't. He never did anything to help my mother and he never appreciated anything she did for him. She just ran around all the time working her fingers to the bone and waiting on him, while he grumbled that the service wasn't up to standard.'

Daniel leaned back in his chair and nodded thoughtfully.

'Yes, that fits,' he murmured.

'Fits what?' demanded Beth in annoyance. 'Whatever are you talking about?'

Daniel's dark eyes narrowed and he smiled unpleasantly. 'It explains the way you behave with Warren,' he said. 'Obviously your role model was your mother. Always anxious to please and never succeeding.'

'That wasn't my role model!' protested Beth hotly, and then bit her lip, an uneasy sensation stirring inside her. The thought had never occurred to her before but was Daniel right? Had it been? Defensively she hit back.

'Why can't you just make polite conversation like normal people?' she demanded.

'I hate polite conversation! It's boring and meaningless.'

'Maybe. But why do you want to know all these odd things about me?'

Daniel shrugged. 'Everybody is moulded by their childhood. I always found when I was dealing with actors that if I could unlock their past I could understand everything about them.'

'Like some kind of party trick?' snapped Beth. 'Well, two can play at that game. What about your parents? Were they happily married?'

Daniel smiled faintly.

'My parents?' he echoed. 'No. My parents weren't happily married, they were happily divorced.'

'Oh,' said Beth, taken aback. 'I'm sorry.'

'Don't be,' replied Daniel. 'It's not an issue for me now, although it was when I was a kid. I remember being very lonely in that big house in Boston with only my father for occasional company.'

She had intended only to hit back, but she found herself suddenly intrigued.

'Your father?' she echoed, wrinkling her nose. 'Why didn't you stay with your mother? Didn't she want you?'

Daniel's eyes took on an expression that made Beth flinch. Hard, ruthless, unforgiving.

'Oh, she wanted me,' he growled. 'But there was a messy custody battle and my father won. He had the money to win.'

'Do you ever see her now?'

The smouldering glint went out of Daniel's eyes and he gave a twisted smile.

'Yes, I do,' he agreed. 'She married again, an assistant professor of history in Iowa, and I have two half-brothers in their early twenties. They're a nice family, but in a way they're not my family, not the way they would have been if I'd grown up with them. But that's all right.'

Something in his tone told Beth that it wasn't all right, that there was still a lot of pent-up anger raging inside him.

'You really hate your father, don't you?' said Beth without thinking.

His reaction was immediate, hostile and uncompromising.

'Don't be a fool!' he snapped. 'That would be giving him far too much importance. But I did hate his values. Money and power were the only things he ever cared about. That, and getting people to do what he wanted. He loved to be in control of things.'

Beth's forehead wrinkled thoughtfully. 'How strange,' she murmured.

'Why? What's strange about it?'

She gave an embarrassed shrug. 'Nothing. Except that he sounds exactly like you.'

Daniel stared at her in outrage. 'Like me?' he snarled. 'That's ridiculous! He was nothing like me.'

Beth remained silent, but continued to watch him with a small, infuriating smile.

'Look,' insisted Daniel angrily, 'I got out from under my father's thumb at the first opportunity! When I was a teenager I made a vow that I was going to make so much money of my own that he'd never be able to control me again.'

'And did you?' asked Beth. 'Or——' She broke off, suddenly realising that what she had been about to ask was in extraordinarily bad taste. After all, it was none of her business whether Daniel had made his obvious wealth himself or inherited it from his father. But she had become absorbed by his story and wanted to know how it ended.

'Or did Daddy put a silver spoon in my mouth?' finished Daniel mockingly. 'No, Beth, Daddy didn't. When I dropped out of Harvard law school at age nineteen, Daddy washed his hands of me. He swore I'd never have another penny out of him and I haven't.'

'Nineteen?' echoed Beth. 'That's young. What did you do? Go and live with your mother?'

Daniel shook his head impatiently.

'No, I didn't want to be a burden to her. I hitch-hiked to Hollywood, of course. Just what any red-blooded kid would do. I wanted to be in the movies.'

'As an actor?' asked Beth.

'No, an actor doesn't have enough control over things. I wanted to be a producer and director.'

Beth smiled mockingly.

'I see,' she murmured. 'You wanted control, did you?'

The unspoken words 'like your father' hovered in the air, but Daniel successfully read her mind.

'No, not like my father!' he exploded. 'Now do you want to hear about this or not?'

'All right, go on,' Beth invited peaceably. 'So you arrived in Hollywood, walked into MGM and said, "I'd like to produce and direct a movie for you," did you?'

Daniel rubbed his forehead as if he were smoothing away a tension headache.

'Well, no, it wasn't quite that easy,' he admitted. 'For two years I worked nights in a hamburger joint as a short-order cook. And in the daytime I worked as an extra on the studio lots whenever I could get hired.'

'Short-order cook?' asked Beth.

'Oh, yes,' agreed Daniel with a short laugh. 'I used to cook a mean hamburger, although it wasn't the sort of talent to impress anyone.'

There was a bitterness in his tone that was oddly jarring. Beth looked at him curiously.

'Were you trying to impress someone?' she asked.

But at that moment the waiter arrived and began setting a plate of fragrant veal and lemon in front of Beth, accompanied by fried potatoes and salad. Daniel looked at the food with relief and shook his head.

'I don't know how the hell you got me started on all that,' he grumbled, picking up his fork. 'I don't usually bore people by telling them the story of my life.'

'I wasn't bored,' insisted Beth.

All the same, she had the feeling that Daniel was glad of the interruption. It's all very well when he's the one firing the questions, she thought shrewdly, but not when he's in the hot seat. It makes him feel too vulnerable. But why? What's he hiding under that all-powerful exterior? Daniel did not speak again until they had both embarked on their main courses. And he seemed to have changed his mind about the boredom of polite conversation. The words 'perfect host' suddenly seemed to be tattooed across his forehead.

'How's the food?' he asked solicitously.

'Great,' said Beth with a faint sigh.

She knew instinctively that his guard was now up, yet somehow she felt as reluctant to drop their earlier discussion as she had been to embark on it. It had been fascinating to learn about Daniel's youth. And, although

he had been rather wary, he hadn't bragged about things
the way Warren always did. She remembered Warren
showing her a photo album of family holidays. 'This is
Mother in Monte Carlo, this is me skiing in Gstaad, this
is my sister Alison at the Cannes Film Festival.' Every
word was designed to impress, but Daniel hadn't done
that. He had simply shared his feelings with her. She
tried to push away her regret that the moment of intimacy was over and simply enjoy her meal. At first she
was successful. The veal was melting and delicious with
its lemony cream sauce and the crispy fried potatoes rich
with bacon and parsley, not to mention the refreshing
green salad. But almost at once Daniel spoiled her
appetite.

'Why did you ever get involved with Warren?' he demanded suddenly. 'Surely those boyish good looks
weren't enough to lure you in, especially when they're
not even accompanied by boyish charm?'

Beth flushed.

'His looks had nothing to do with it,' she retorted.

But even as she spoke she knew it wasn't quite true.
Warren's looks had formed a part, although only a very
small part, of her complex reasons for becoming involved with him. Her eyes took on a tormented expression as she cast her mind back to that time three
years ago. She remembered it all so vividly. Her brother
Andrew, newly qualified as a doctor, had insisted on
paying for a really slap-up twenty-first birthday party
for her and his girlfriend Sue had entered into the spirit
of things by offering her parents' home as a venue. They
were away overseas. What could be more suitable? But
Beth had found herself in the embarrassing position of
not having enough guests to invite to the party. Being
hard-working and rather shy, she only had four or five
close friends and to bolster the numbers she had

impulsively asked Warren. After all they had worked together on a third-term project and knew each other slightly. But there certainly hadn't been any great romance. Not then. And if it hadn't been for a deeply disturbing incident at the party she might never have got to know Warren any better.

At the moment when her mother was already halfway through lighting candles on the cake someone had realised that Beth's brother-in-law, Greg, was missing. She remembered how she had offered to go and fetch him and then had frugally blown out the candles that were already lit. It was rather like an omen when you thought about it. As if only half her wishes were going to come true. What had she wished for, anyway? Love? Success? She could no longer remember. But she did remember finding Greg in the rumpus-room which opened out on to the swimming-pool on the lower level of the house. He was alone and must have just come out of the pool, for his body was streaming with water and he was clad only in bathing trunks. An unwilling pang of desire had shot through her at the sight of that dark, powerful figure and she was conscious of an unwelcome tremor in her voice when she spoke.

'Greg, we're ready to cut the cake now.'

He had smiled at her slowly, lazily.

'Well, good. Do I get a kiss from the birthday girl then?'

Before she had time to protest he had swept her into his arms and kissed her. Not on the cheek but full on her open mouth. And to Beth's horror for the merest fraction of a second she had responded, kissing him back with inexperienced fervour. A moment later, hating herself, she had broken away, flushed and trembling. Bolting back up the stairs, she had run straight into Warren who had come to look for her. Warren had seemed so safe, so normal, unthreatening. Somehow it had all started from that moment. Daniel's harsh voice broke into her thoughts.

'I asked you why you became involved with Warren,' he said.

She took in a swift, unsteady breath.

'Because he seemed safe,' she replied.

'Safe,' mocked Daniel. 'That seems an odd reason to start a relationship. Unless——' His dark eyes narrowed thoughtfully. 'Unless you were on the rebound from somebody totally unsafe.' Too shocked even to lie, Beth cast him a stricken look. 'How did you guess?' she whispered.

His laugh was nothing but a mirthless growl. 'You forget that I spent years as a film director,' he replied. 'In that job you learn to read people's faces. Bodies are often more honest than speech and your body tells me something that you don't even want to admit to yourself.'

'What's that?' queried Beth unwisely.

Daniel caught her fingers in a merciless grip and held them.

'That you're not the kind of woman who was born to live safely,' he retorted. 'You're a person who was born to take risks, to live life to the full. You're doing violence to your own nature by staying with a pathetic creature like Warren.'

Beth snatched away her fingers as if they had been burned. 'Surely that's for me to decide?' she snapped.

Daniel's expression was as brooding as a thundercloud. 'Not if I have anything to do with it,' he muttered.

'But you don't have anything to do with it, do you? It's none of your damned business.'

Daniel changed his tack. Helping himself to more salad, he eyed her thoughtfully under lowered lids.

'Tell me,' he said, 'how do you like the United States?'

Beth consciously had to take a deep breath and relax. She realised that her body was tensed up ready for fight or flight and instead he had suddenly thrown a simple question at her. So simple that it was unexpected. She shrugged expressively.

'Well, what I've seen of it is very nice, which isn't much. I haven't even been to Disneyland yet. But I think California is wonderful. I love the climate and in many ways it reminds me of home. And the people are really friendly and dynamic. I think it's a great place.'

'Would you ever consider living here?'

The question shot out so rapidly that it took her by surprise. For a moment a wild thought rose in her head only to be instantly dismissed.

'You mean for business reasons?' she asked.

Daniel smiled thinly. 'All right, let's say for business reasons. Would you consider living here?'

Beth turned the idea over. 'Yes, I think I'd probably enjoy it,' she admitted. 'If I were earning enough to live comfortably.'

'You wouldn't miss your family?' asked Daniel.

She smiled affectionately. 'Not if I could see them at least once a year,' she agreed. 'My mother is retired now and Andrew bought her a home unit down at Cronulla near the beach. She's got a life of her own, going to bowls and doing things with Kerry's children. And I'm fond of my sister and brother but we never really spent a great deal of time together. Yes, I think if the chance came my way I'd jump at it. After all, the United States is one of the most important fashion places in the world.'

'And fashion is what you care about most?' asked Daniel.

Beth's eyes clouded.

'It is at the moment,' she agreed. 'You see, I have to earn my living and I really like to do the very best I can at anything I tackle. But putting it like that gives it far too much importance somehow. I mean, you'd have to be an awfully superficial person to think that fashion was the most important thing in your life, wouldn't you?'

Daniel shot her a piercing look.

'So what do you think ought to be the most important thing your life?' he demanded.

Beth wriggled, feeling uncomfortable at this inquisition. But the steadiness of his gaze demanded an answer.

'I don't know. A home, a family if I ever had one,' she replied huskily. 'I can't think of anything much more important than that.'

His eyes strayed to the mysterious envelope on the table. 'I'm pleased to hear it,' he said mockingly. 'You sound like a positive paragon of womanhood.'

She dropped her gaze, hating him for making fun of her, hating herself for giving him the opportunity. With a vague feeling of surprise she realised that her plate was empty.

'Would you like a pudding?' asked Daniel.

'I suppose so,' she agreed in a subdued voice.

The zabaglione was heavenly, a warm, bittersweet froth of Marsala and beaten egg yolk. And the cappuccino which followed it was equally good with its thick, creamy layer of foam and chocolate. But Beth barely tasted them. The thought that she was never going to see Daniel again cast a shadow over the meal, because the truth was that she would miss him. And in some ways the most hurtful feature of this dinner was the manila envelope which lay between them on the table like the boundary marker in a tug-o'-war. Somehow it reduced all that had happened between them to a sterile business transaction, and Beth could not help finding her gaze drawn towards it with a mixture of resentment and fascination. At last, when the empty cups had been removed, Daniel picked it up and handed it to her.

His eyes were dark, piercing, inescapable. She felt they were boring right through to her soul. Try as she might, she could not turn away.

'I said this was a farewell dinner,' he said. 'But it doesn't have to be a farewell. It's up to you.'

An incredulous joy flooded through her, followed rapidly by suspicion and misgiving.

'What do you mean?' she demanded sharply.

'I have a proposition to put to you,' he said.

'What kind of a proposition?'

'Have a look through the letter and the documents and then I'll explain everything.'

With trembling fingers she opened the envelope and scanned its contents. It was written on the letterhead of a firm of lawyers and it began with the words 'Dear Miss Saxon', but after that it was such gibberish that it might as well have been written in Greek. Full of words like 'whereas' and 'heretofore'. With a puzzled sound she put the letter at the back and looked through the accompanying documents. It was some kind of contract. But her head swam when she tried to understand it. An incredulous notion rose in her head.

'You mean you want to go into business with me formally?' she asked. 'Employ me and eventually form a company? Called Solo Designs?'

Daniel nodded.

'But why?' demanded Beth. 'And how? Wouldn't I have to get a work permit? And what if I went broke? You'd lose heaps of money. And where could I make the clothes? I can't keep living at your place forever.'

Daniel smiled, but the smile did not reach his eyes which were lit with a strange brooding glint.

'You can leave all the details to me,' he said impatiently. 'If necessary, I'll move mountains to allow you to stay in the United States. And as for going bankrupt, don't give it a thought, Beth. I won't allow it to happen. You're going places, girl. And you're going there with me.'

She stared at him in disbelief, feeling half elated, half terrified.

'But where would I work?' she asked.

'That's easy,' he said. 'I have a horse farm just near Buellton with an old barn that's not being used. I could easily fix it up as a factory for you. And there are local girls nearby who could work for you. Wendy Fulton, for one. I'll take you up tomorrow to see the place if you're interested.'

Beth hesitated. Belatedly she remembered that she wasn't alone in her fashion venture.

'I'd have to see what Warren thinks,' she began, but Daniel cut her off sharply.

'Warren won't be involved. You might as well get one thing straight, Beth. If you accept my offer, there's no place for Warren in this business.'

CHAPTER SIX

ALL Beth's old fears came rushing back to torment her. Daniel's offer seemed far too good to be true, so why was he making it? She thought of his passionate kisses in the conservatory and then of his offhand behaviour at the lunch. And she looked down at the contract dangling between her fingers as if it were some kind of loathsome spider.

'Why are you offering me this?' she asked suspiciously.

'Not to get you into my bed, if that's what you think,' he snapped. 'There are no hidden traps in that document, Beth. And you're perfectly free to take it to an attorney or an agent and get it checked out. In fact, I advise you to do so.'

Beth hesitated, feeling a confused mixture of emotions. She could no longer deny that she was violently attracted to Daniel. Whenever she looked at him she felt a hollow ache inside that was close to physical pain, and the corrosive jealousy she had felt on seeing him with Sunny earlier in the day made it even clearer to her how deeply he stirred her. But those weren't good reasons to get involved with him. Far from it. As far as Beth was concerned they were reasons for running miles in the opposite direction.

Even worse was the high-handed way he was trying to turn her against Warren. All right, maybe Warren wasn't perfect, but Beth was an adult and had an adult's right to choose her own associates. How dared Daniel try and dictate to her about telling Warren to leave? And why was he doing it? Did he simply want to seduce her without any opposition? She cast him a tormented look.

'But Warren helped design the collection!' she protested. 'You can't just leave him out of the deal.'

'I can and I will,' retorted Daniel.

The stormy glint in his eye and the aggressive angle of his chin didn't invite argument, but Beth was naturally stubborn. Besides which, she had a strong sense of justice.

'It wouldn't be fair!' she insisted. 'Warren and I planned this collection together, so surely he's entitled to some share in the profits?'

'Maybe,' muttered Daniel grudgingly. 'Although I can't say I ever saw him do any work. I'll call my attorney and have him offer a generous payment for any designs Warren did. But that's the last time I have any dealings with the guy. And the same rule will apply to you if you're my employee. You'll have nothing more to do with him. Is that clear, Beth?'

She stared at him in outrage. 'Do you mean professionally or privately?' she demanded.

'Both.'

A gasp of indignation momentarily choked Beth. 'You can't control my private life!' she exclaimed furiously.

'Maybe not,' conceded Daniel with regret. 'But I sure as hell can control this company I plan to form. And Warren won't be involved in it.'

'Why not?' Beth persisted.

'Because he's a parasite!' growled Daniel. 'And I don't offer handouts to freeloaders. I'm satisfied that you're a genuine worker, but Warren isn't. If you let him get in on the act, he'll only cause you trouble by throwing his weight around and not performing. That's why I don't want him.'

'Th-that's the only reason?' stammered Beth, eyeing him intently.

Daniel's lips parted in a feral smile.

'Sure. What other reason could there be? I know the guy thinks he's your bodyguard and he'd like to knock my teeth out, but I'm not afraid of him. And I'm not offering you this contract because I want to make love to you.'

Beth flinched. An uneasy emotion seeped through her which should have been relief, but which felt oddly like disappointment.

'I see,' she said with a small, tight smile.

Daniel's mocking dark eyes met hers and he leaned across the table towards her. An invisible current seemed to spark between them and Beth shrank.

'Don't misunderstand me,' he added throatily. 'I do want to make love to you, but the contract is a separate issue. It's not dependent on that.'

Beth felt a jolt of mingled shock and excitement at his frankness. Forgetting all about being sophisticated and worldly, she stared at him with a stunned expression.

'What did you say?' she whispered.

'I said the contract is a separate issue,' repeated Daniel slowly and deliberately.

Colour flooded her cheeks.

'Don't make me play games,' she implored. 'I mean . . . the other thing you said.'

Every line in his body seemed to radiate purpose and raw sensual energy. His dark eyebrows were drawn together, his eyes glittered and beneath the powerful, predatory curve of his nose his mouth was set in a determined line.

'You know what I want from you,' he said hoarsely. 'You want the same from me—but you won't admit it.' His mouth hardened. 'You may be damn good at your

job, Beth, but in your private life you're gutless, inde-
cisive and cowardly.'

Beth stared at him open-mouthed for several seconds,
too angry for words. Then at last she found her voice.

'How dare you?' she demanded shakily.

'You know I'm telling the truth! You only stay with
Warren because someone once hurt you and you haven't
the courage to pick yourself up and risk being hurt again.
That's pretty spineless, isn't it?'

Beth's indignation boiled over. She sprang to her feet.
'I'm leaving,' she said.

Daniel seized her wrist and hauled her back into the
chair. 'Sit down,' he ordered. 'I haven't finished with
you.'

'Well, I've finished with you!' blazed Beth.

'No, you haven't,' Daniel insisted, still holding her
wrist. 'You may think so but you're wrong. Oh, you can
take this contract away and show it to half a dozen
agents, and I hope you will, but in the end you'll sign
it. I'm one hundred per cent sure of that.'

Beth's blue eyes blazed.

'Give me one good reason why I should!' she
challenged.

A secretive, triumphant smile flickered around the
edges of Daniel's mouth.

'Because you're not the only one who'll suffer if you
don't. You've made commitments to other people. And
you can't let them down, can you? What about your
poor mother who gave you money she could ill afford
to let you come over here?'

'You'd actually use that kind of emotional blackmail?'
demanded Beth contemptuously.

'I'd use anything I had to in order to convince you,'
he retorted. 'But it's in your own best interests, Beth. I

don't want you to miss an opportunity that won't come your way again in a hurry.'

'I'll bet,' muttered Beth stormily.

'Look,' said Daniel, pointing his forefinger at her as if it were a loaded gun, 'you've got a lot of talent and it would be a hell of shame if you wasted it. It's my job to see that you don't.'

'So you're just going to organise my life for me from now on, are you?'

'That's right. And if you had any brains you'd be grateful. I've often been told I bring out the best in people.'

Beth ground her teeth.

'Does bringing out the best in people include making them commit murder with a table-knife?' she demanded.

Daniel raised one eyebrow lazily.

'I don't think you'd go that far,' he said. 'But at least I'd be dying in a good cause. Come on, Beth. Accept my offer.'

'I'll think about it,' muttered Beth ungraciously.

'Good,' said Daniel suavely.

Up until this moment he had radiated an explosive, threatening energy, as if he were passionately involved in Beth's decision. Yet now, with a rapidity that baffled her, his intensity evaporated. He rose to his feet as genially as if this were nothing more than a routine business discussion. 'You don't have to decide right now about the contract. Call your agent and talk to her about it. If you're interested, I'll drive you up to the farm tomorrow afternoon so you can see the place for yourself. What do you say?'

'All right,' said Beth uncertainly. 'Thank you.'

All the way home in the car she sat in silence, but her feelings were in turmoil. She couldn't deny being strongly tempted by Daniel's business offer, however much he infuriated her. The chance to stay on in America and market her fashion designs was almost too good to be true. Yet a perverse sense of pride urged her to refuse it. She didn't relish the idea of being under an obligation to a man like Daniel Pryor, a man who not only radiated a sensuality that was deeply unsettling, but also told her quite frankly that he wanted to make love to her. The whole situation was disturbing and yet shockingly enticing. Still, if she only had herself to consider, she would certainly opt for safety and run for her life. But Daniel had shrewdly targeted her greatest weakness—her loyalty to others. How could she ever explain to her mother that she had passed up an opportunity like this? It was unthinkable! Besides, she had no real proof that Daniel was a casual womaniser, cynically using his charms to seduce any girl that took his fancy. Even his apparent flirtation with Sunny Martino this morning might have been no more than a product of Beth's overheated imagination. Perhaps he was really quite safe after all? Yet when they reached the apartment building Beth had another shock. Daniel pulled up outside the front door and handed her a key.

'I'm not likely to be home tonight,' he explained. 'I have some business affairs to see to. So just help yourself to anything you need in the apartment. I'll pick you up tomorrow afternoon around two to take you to the farm.'

'Just as you like.'

Beth's lips set in a cynical, quivering line as she strode past the doorman into the building. Business affairs, she thought bitterly as she rode up in the lift. I'll bet! Business with Sunny Martino, I suppose.

Her hands were shaking as she unlocked the door to the apartment, but she tried fiercely to regain control of herself. After all, what did it have to do with her if Daniel spent the night with his girlfriend? She would do much better to try and figure out where her own relationship with Warren was headed. Yet try as she might, her tired brain refused to handle the subject sensibly. Whenever she tried to think of Warren, her imagination kept winging back to Daniel and she found it strangely difficult to remember how much she disapproved of him. All she could think of was the deep, pulsating excitement of his kisses and the agonised sense of betrayal she had felt on seeing him with Sunny. And when she reminded herself that she had spent three years with Warren, that she felt safe as his fiancée, that he had always sworn he would actually marry her one of these days, she could only remember one thing: how he had gone away and left her when she was in difficulties. 'Men are such swine!' she groaned, thumping the pillow. 'I don't want to have anything to do with either of them!'

Yet in spite of that resolution she woke the following morning with a sense of anticipation. While she ate breakfast, her thoughts kept straying back to Daniel's business proposition, and at last she gave in and decided to phone her agent. Hesitantly she read out the letter and explained the terms of the contract.

'Beth, you'd be crazy not to accept that,' insisted Leonie forcefully. 'It's the chance of a lifetime. Grab it with both hands.'

'Are you sure?' asked Beth.

'Yes, I'm sure,' said Leonie. 'Do it now.'

Beth's next phone call was even harder to make. Although she still felt tormented and confused, she was sure of one thing: that she needed time off from her relationship with Warren to work out where she was going and what she really wanted in life. Hesitating with the receiver in her hand, she ran through the arguments which had been buzzing in her head all night. Do I still want to marry Warren, even supposing I could get him to marry me? She tried to tell herself she did. Yet deep down she knew it was no longer true, although once it had been. She could remember furious arguments on the subject. Tears, cajoling, pleading on her part. Sulking and evasion on Warren's. But now for the first time she admitted to herself what she had always known, deep down. He just doesn't think I'm good enough for him. And if he's not going to marry me, do I want to go on having a relationship with him at all?

Her answer to that was much clearer, rising like a cry from the depths of her heart. No! In some strange way she knew it was a result of Daniel's having kissed her, although she couldn't explain why. But now the thought of Warren touching her seemed horrifying. Like a violation. And, quite apart from her own irrational feelings on the subject, wasn't it unfair to Warren to expect him to stay with her when she was so obsessed by Daniel? So what was the point of continuing the relationship at all? No, the only sensible thing to do was to end it. Warren would be offended, of course; he had a violent temper and a poisonous tongue when he was enraged, but she would simply have to face that. And oddly the thought didn't frighten her as much as she expected, perhaps because some of Daniel's abrasive readiness to jump in and attack problems had rubbed off on her. Whatever the reason, she felt a strange new courage that allowed her to tackle the unthinkable.

Taking a deep breath, she made up her mind. With jerky, anxious movements she picked up the telephone and punched in the numbers of the motel where Warren was staying.

'Hello, Starlight Motel.'

'May I speak to Mr Warren Clark, please?'

'One moment, madam. I'll put you through.'

A girl's voice answered the phone, sleepy and rather slurred. 'Hi, who is it?'

'I'm sorry,' said Beth hastily. 'They must have put me through to the wrong room. I wanted Mr Warren Clark.'

There was a muffled yawn. 'Oh, he's here, just a minute.'

An incredible suspicion flashed through Beth's mind and a moment later Warren came on the line, his voice wary.

'Hello, Warren Clark speaking.'

'Warren, it's Beth.'

Silence. It should have been a heartbroken, agonised silence. After all, even an imbecile could guess what was going on, and yet Beth was surprised to find that, apart from a faint bitter sense of betrayal, her main emotion was one of relief. He's found someone else, she thought in amazement, so I don't have to feel guilty or afraid that I'm hurting him.

Then Warren spoke.

'Oh, hi, Beth,' he said with false heartiness. 'Look, don't go jumping to any wrong conclusions, will you? I can explain——'

Beth cut him off short.

'Please don't bother, Warren,' she said in a rapid, staccato voice. 'I'm just ringing to tell you that I think we should end our relationship. It's obviously not going anywhere and I need time to sort out what I want.'

'Beth, wait!' shouted Warren. 'Look, just because of some one-night stand that doesn't mean a damn thing, you don't have to go destroying an entire relationship!'

'It's not because of that,' insisted Beth hastily. 'I'd already made up my mind! It's because I don't really love you, Warren. I thought I did, but I was wrong and I don't believe that you love me either. It's over. Don't you see? Over.'

'No, I don't,' said Warren hotly. 'Beth——'

'Don't make this any harder for both of us,' she begged. 'I hope it works out for you with this girl, I really do. And that you enjoy the trade shows in New York. I won't be going myself, so I'll say goodbye now.'

'Beth, wait! Why aren't you going to New York? What the hell's going on? You can't just dump me like this after three years! Why don't we——?'

'Goodbye, Warren,' she repeated hoarsely. 'Please don't try to contact me.'

And with a swift convulsive movement she replaced the receiver. At first an absurd sense of betrayal and anticlimax filled her entire body, and yet, when she had showered and dressed, she found that she did not feel as bad as she had expected. Perhaps it was only the inevitable pain of admitting that she had made a mistake and finding the courage for a new beginning. Beth's smile twisted wryly. Well, this time she was determined about one thing. Finding out about Warren's sly affair simply confirmed her low opinion of men. So from now on she wasn't going to take any more risks. No other man was going to entice her into a love-affair, however attractive he might be.

As he had promised, Daniel arrived back shortly after two p.m. the following afternoon to drive her to the farm. Beth had spent several difficult hours trying to puzzle out what her attitude towards him should be. After all, if she did decide to work for him, there was no future in outright antagonism. Nor could she allow too much intimacy to develop. In the end she resolved that an attitude of aloof friendliness was best.

Unfortunately her resolve was tested from the very first moment. As Daniel strode whistling into the apartment, she noticed that he had changed out of his dinner suit of the previous evening into a pair of shorts and striped polo-shirt, and a pang of resentment shot through her. No doubt he kept a suitable supply of clothes on hand at Sunny Martino's home! Well, it was nothing to do with her, she reminded herself. Daniel might have lured her into a momentary madness once, but never again. From now on the relationship between them would be strictly business.

It was just after four o'clock in the afternoon when they reached Daniel's farm in the Santa Ynez Valley just outside Buellton. The sky was an intense, cloudless blue and the tawny hills with their sun-bleached grass and scattering of eucalypt trees reminded Beth of Australia. As Daniel turned the Jaguar into a gravelled driveway she had a vivid impression of coming home. A white Spanish-style gateway with a huge black bell set in the centre of it loomed up ahead of them and Daniel pressed a button, causing the gate to swing open in front of them.

Rolling down the window, Beth put her head out and looked eagerly around her. There was a red rambling rose hanging over the gateway and the warm perfume of its flowers mingled with the scent of newly mown grass. Turning her head a little, she saw that a teenage boy was mowing the grass strip which divided the driveway into two. He paused at their approach, grinned and waved a hand in greeting.

'That's Jake Kronborg, the manager's son,' explained Daniel.

Beth nodded, looking around her with interest.

'Are all these horses yours?' she asked in awe.

On either side of the road were large, fenced pastures thick and lush with grass. And in these horses were grazing peacefully or standing in the shade of the spreading trees.

'Most of them,' agreed Daniel. 'About a hundred and fifty are mine. The others I agist for various people.'

'And was it all set up like this when you bought it?' asked Beth, waving her hand at the luxuriant pastures, the tree-lined driveway and the cluster of cream stuccoed buildings that was just coming into view at the end of the drive. Daniel smiled briefly.

'No, it was all just tomato fields and flower fields back then,' he replied. 'Not even a tree in sight. And no buildings apart from an old barn and a ruined farmhouse. A lot of back-breaking work went into making the place the way you see it today.'

On either side of the driveway was an avenue of huge deodar trees and as the car glided over the gravel they passed through an alternating pattern of light and shade until at last they came out into a huge turning circle in front of the house. In the centre of this was a signpost with signs pointing in various directions—'Office', 'Training Center', 'Breeding Barn', 'Visitors' Car Park'— but Daniel ignored these and drove right up to the house itself. Climbing out, Beth gazed around her with reluctant fascination. Secretly she was half hoping for something to be hopelessly wrong with Daniel's business proposal so that she could escape from the whole situation. Of course, she would rather walk barefoot over hot coals than tell him the true reason for her misgivings: that she found the sexual tension between them unbearable. Yet if there were some practical problem with the whole project she could still back out with her pride intact. If only the building were in ruins or labour impossible to hire or deliveries too difficult, what a relief it would be! But, to Beth's despair, the place seemed absolutely perfect.

The main house itself was rather like Daniel's villa in Santa Barbara, although smaller. It was faced with a cream-coloured stucco and roofed with orange pantiles and there was a loggia running along the front of the house to offer protection from the sun. Yellow gazanias and white African daisies grew in profusion in the flowerbeds and the air was filled with the scent of cut grass, horses and eucalyptus trees. To the left of the house Beth could see the outline of several large barns and as she watched a van drove out of one of these and came past them. A man in a cowboy hat raised his hand to them from the driver's seat.

'That's the farrier,' explained Daniel.

Beth saw that there was a small portable furnace and anvil in the back of the van. Stepping inside the loggia, Daniel rang the large iron bell that was set in a niche. A moment later a tall man of about forty appeared. He was blond, with very light blue eyes, and wore jeans and a checked shirt.

'Beth, this is my farm manager, Eric Kronborg,' Daniel announced. 'Eric, I'd like you to meet Beth Saxon. She may be opening a business in our disused barn here.'

'Hi, Beth,' said Eric, wiping his large hand on his jeans before he extended it to her.

'Hello, Eric.'

'Is Jenny anywhere about?' asked Daniel.

'Sure. She's in the breeding barn,' agreed Eric. 'Would you like me to take you over?'

'No, we'll find our own way, thanks,' said Daniel.

He led Beth on a short-cut over the green, closely trimmed lawn between red Chinese fire bushes and clumps of Texas privet. After the brilliant sunlight outside, the gloom of the barn was dazzling and for a moment Beth blinked, unable to see. She heard the soft whinny of the mare, the shuffle of hoofs in the dust and smelt a strong aroma of hay and horse dung. Then suddenly her eyes grew accustomed to the shadows and she saw a slightly built dark-haired woman hurrying towards them down the aisle between the pens.

'Daniel!' cried the woman eagerly. 'What a lovely surprise! And who's this?'

'Jenny, this is Beth Saxon. Beth, Jenny Kronborg, Eric's wife.'

Briefly Daniel explained what he and Beth were doing there and Jenny nodded enthusiastically.

'Well, bring Beth back to the house for coffee when you're finished showing her around, won't you?' she urged. 'But before you leave, you must come and have a look at how your baby is getting on, Daniel.'

Beth cast Jenny a startled glance. Daniel's baby? But a moment later she understood as Jenny made her way to one of the wide pens, crouched down beside it and crooned softly to a small bright-eyed animal inside.

'Oh!' cried Beth in delight. 'It's not even a foal. It's a baby deer.'

Daniel came and joined her, leaning against the pen so that his body loomed over her. He was so close that his knee was almost touching her back.

'Yes, I found him a couple of months ago,' he said. 'His mother had been killed by a car and the poor little guy was wandering around terrified on the highway, dazzled by the headlights. It was only a matter of time before he got run over too or died of starvation, so I brought him here to Jenny.'

Jenny glanced up at him with exasperated affection and rose slowly to her feet.

'Daniel can never resist a lame dog, Beth,' she warned. 'I thought the poor little thing had had it, but Daniel insisted that we try, so we did. We couldn't get him to feed from a bottle, but in the end one of our nanny-goats adopted him. Now he's bigger than she is, but he still doesn't want to be parted from her.'

Beth peered in more closely through the wire mesh and followed Jenny's pointing finger. She saw that a dainty white goat was huddled near the back of the pen. As she watched, the animal came forward and gave the fawn an affectionate nudge.

'Well, time we got moving,' urged Daniel.

As she followed Daniel around one of the gravel paths Beth pondered on what she had just seen. She couldn't help being touched by the odd story of the deer and its unusual foster mother, but at the same time it surprised her. She wouldn't have thought of Daniel as the kind of man to care about an orphaned and abandoned animal. He was too ruthless, too forceful, too closely focused on success and achievement. So had he been acting out of character the night he rescued the fawn or was there a side to his character that she knew nothing about?

Daniel led her through an archway in a hedge of Japanese privet and they came out in front of another Spanish villa with a panoramic view of the golden valley and the blue hills beyond.

'That's the house I live in when I'm here,' he said, waving a careless hand at it. 'And your cottage is along the road there beyond those cypresses.'

'My cottage?' echoed Beth in bewilderment.

'The original farmhouse,' explained Daniel. 'But don't worry, it's been fixed up and made habitable. I thought it would be easiest and pleasantest for you to live here on the site. And it's not far to Santa Barbara or Los Angeles. You'd be able to get down to your shops easily enough, once I buy you a car.'

'Sh-shops?' stammered Beth uncertainly.

'Yes, didn't I tell you? I'm planning one in Los Angeles and one in Santa Barbara. You'll need some upmarket retail outlets for clothes like yours.'

The feeling that she was drowning came over Beth almost as forcefully as it had at their first meeting. It seemed that nothing would suffice for Daniel except a total reorganisation of her life. A snap of his fingers, a few words of command and she would have a new home, a new car, a new business and a lifestyle to match. Could he possibly do all that for her and want nothing in return except some dubious profits from her designs? It seemed wildly unlikely, and Beth found all her old suspicions resurrected. She was so busy panicking about whether Daniel was going to sweep her into a torrid embrace in a back bedroom that she noticed very little in their tour of the cottage. Vaguely she had the impression of a rustic charm which would respond well to decorating. But by now she had completely made up her mind. Any benefits that might flow from accepting Daniel's offer simply weren't worth the emotional risk of making a fool of herself or losing her self-respect. All she wanted to do now was find a suitable chance to tell him and get the ordeal over.

'The cottage is very nice,' she said abruptly. 'But can't we look at the barn? That's what I really need to see.'

With long, energetic strides he led the way through an overgrown garden to a tumbledown fence. Then he paused and held down a wire for Beth to clamber over.

'This is it,' he said, gesturing at a building that was half smothered in a tangled growth of fragrant honeysuckle. 'Try to picture it not as it is but the way it could be. I can have the floor fixed and put in the right equipment and lighting for you.'

She should have been delighted, for here at last was her cast-iron alibi, her excuse for throwing up her hands in despair over the whole project. And yet perversely Beth's heart sank as she entered the building. It was made of wood with two huge doors at one end and it must have been over ninety years old. When Daniel flung open one of the doors with a protesting squeak, and bright sunlight flooded the interior, she saw that the cobwebs were hanging thickly from blackened rafters and that the floor was only of dirt. Along one side was a row of loose boxes and old feeding troughs and at the far end was another door.

'That's the old tack-room through there,' said Daniel. 'You could use that as an office. The building is on the level which will be good for deliveries and there's plenty of space for storage and equipment. Come through and see the rest of it.'

The tack-room windows had tiny panes of glass which were cracked and filthy with dust. There was a wooden floor but one of the planks had rotted through, leaving a hole the size of a man's foot. And the fireplace in one wall was filled with dead leaves. Even the air in the room smelt musty and old.

'Well, what do you think?' asked Daniel. 'The place has possibilities, doesn't it?'

Beth stifled a groan. As far as she could see the only possibility the place had was that of falling down or being bulldozed.

'Yes, I suppose so,' she said doubtfully.

Daniel let out a low growl of laughter. Then he stepped forward and took her face in his hands.

'The trouble with you, young woman,' he said huskily, 'is that you don't let your imagination run away with you enough.'

Beth felt an ache of shocked excitement quiver through her entire body at the touch of his hands. In that instant her senses grew unbearably sharpened, so that she felt acutely conscious of the ticking of the watch on Daniel's wrist, the heat radiating out of his body, the dark mat of hair visible through the open neck of his shirt. And she found she had no difficulty whatsoever in letting her imagination run away with her, except that she was appalled by the images that it produced. A wanton, sensual

kaleidoscope of pictures danced before her eyes. She imagined Daniel letting his hands trail down from her cheeks on to her shoulders and down over the swelling mounds of her breasts and then she thought of how she would unbutton his shirt and slide her hands inside, feel the warm, muscular hardness of his chest and then...
She shuddered, firmly reining in her imagination. Daniel looked at her with a strange, sardonic tilt of his black eyebrows as if he were reading her mind.

'Don't give it up as impossible,' he urged in a low voice.

Shock and embarrassment flooded through her and then she realised belatedly that he was only talking about the transformation of the barn. Hastily she backed out of his hold.

'Well, I can't help thinking——' she began uneasily.

But he was already talking again. 'The barn's no problem, I can have that fixed in two weeks, but the rest of it needs your touch, Beth, your designs. There aren't a whole lot of people I would trust with a project like this...'

She took in a long, unsteady breath, feeling as if an abyss were opening under her feet.

'But if you're too scared to take the risk...' Daniel continued.

Beth hesitated, bit her lip, stared at him suspiciously. He might be telling the truth, in which case she felt strangely reluctant to lose his good opinion of her. Or he might not. But she suddenly realised that she didn't care, because she wanted to do this, risky or not. A soft gasp of laughter overtook her.

'No, I'm not scared, Daniel!' she retorted. 'And I am going to take the risk. But on one condition.'

'What's that?'

She flushed and then looked at him directly.

'That the relationship between us is strictly business. Nothing more.'

His gaze slid down over her body with a touch of mockery.

'Whatever you say, ma'am,' he replied provocatively. 'But if you ever change your mind, just let me know.'

CHAPTER SEVEN

BETH was furiously certain that she wouldn't change her mind, but it wasn't as easy as she had expected to stick to that decision. The more she got to know Daniel Pryor, the more he disconcerted her. And the worst part about it was that he never seemed to play by any recognisable rules. At first she thought she had him safely catalogued and filed. 'Class "A" Wolf—Not to Be Trusted.' As he stormed around California like a whirlwind setting up her business, she had ample opportunity to see his careless charm in action. Every time Daniel had dealings with a female between the ages of eight and eighty, the husky voice, the smouldering brown eyes, the resolute refusal to take 'no' for an answer always came into play. And it made Beth grind her teeth in annoyance to see how effective it was. Women fell all over themselves to do what he wanted. How can they be so gullible? she asked herself a dozen times a day. If it comes to that, how can I be? She began to regret her weakness in giving in to Daniel's bullying. Or sweet talk. Or manipulation. Or whatever it was that had made her temporarily lose her mind and agree to work for him.

Yet at the same time an innate sense of justice forced her to admit that Daniel really was working incredibly hard on her behalf. Within days he seemed to have moved heaven and earth to get her business up and running. His first action was to take her to Santa Barbara to do a new set of photographs to replace those lost in the launch accident. He offered his yacht as the venue for the photographs and to Beth's surprise suggested that he should take them himself, telling her, 'Back when I decided to become a movie director, I studied courses in photography and cinematography. I thought I could get the best work out of my cameramen if I knew what they should be doing.'

'All right,' agreed Beth. 'Thank you.'

Just before sunrise the next morning with Benson at the helm of the big yacht they sailed out into the harbour and Daniel set to work. For nearly two hours he put Beth through her paces, taking roll after roll of film. And apart from directing her on how to pose he scarcely spoke the entire time. Yet towards the end of the session he suddenly began to talk.

As he turned her profile carefully towards the hills so that the rising sun was coming out in a great nimbus of light around her shoulders, he said in a casual tone, 'You're a remarkably good-looking young woman, you know. When did you reach your full height?'

Beth sighed.

'At thirteen.'

'I bet you had the boys clustering around you like flies.'

'You must be joking,' replied Beth with a snort of laughter. 'Five feet eight and thirteen years old! I felt like a freak on stilts. The one big prayer of my teenage years was that somebody would ask me to dance with him, but nobody ever did.'

'Until Prince Charming in the form of Warren came along,' grated Daniel. 'Well, I can almost understand why you felt insecure as a teenager. But don't you think it's time you got over it now?'

'I'm not insecure!' retorted Beth defensively.

'Of course you are,' insisted Daniel. 'Hell, you acted like a whipped puppy when Warren came to see you the day after I met you.'

Beth drew in an outraged breath, but said nothing.

'Don't bare your teeth like that, sweetheart, you're wrecking my photo.'

Good! thought Beth, and then remembered belatedly that it was also *her* photo, intended to advertise *her* fashion collection. Besides, there was such a thing as dignity and she saw no point in being drawn into an undignified squabble. With a heroic effort she fought down her rage and smiled sweetly at the camera. Daniel looked disappointed.

'Say something,' he urged. 'Tell me what you think about my brilliant, insightful analysis of your character.'

Beth was goaded into a scathing retort.

'I think your brilliant, insightful analysis is full of...' Hastily she stopped short and clamped her lips shut. But her blue eyes continued to shoot fire.

'Tsk, tsk,' muttered Daniel. 'Do proper young ladies like you really use language like that?'

'I didn't!' flared Beth.

'No, but I wish you had,' said Daniel regretfully. 'You're too uptight, Beth. Always worrying about what you should say and what you should feel. Too scared to take risks. But you ought to take risks, you ought to say what you think.'

'One of these days I'll say what I think about you,' threatened Beth in a dangerous voice.

A smile curved Daniel's lips.

'Do that!' he urged. 'I'll look forward to it.'

'Even if I lose my temper?' scoffed Beth.

'Especially if you lose your temper. If you ever begin to assert yourself, you'll be dynamite. I only hope I'm there to see it.'

'Well, you won't be!' vowed Beth.

With the energy and thoroughness that characterised everything he did, Daniel had the photos developed and printed the same afternoon so that they were able to examine them over dinner. Rather to Beth's surprise, they turned out to be excellent. Luminous, vivid and completely unforgettable, they brought out the drama of the clothes, but also lent Beth an ethereal grace which she hadn't known she possessed. She spent a long time gazing at them and felt oddly perturbed by them. Why? she wondered. Was it because the word which best described them didn't seem to have any associations with Daniel? 'Sensitive'.

'What is it?' he asked, watching her intently. 'Don't you like them?'

Beth shook her head with a puzzled frown.

'It's not that at all,' she said sincerely. 'They're wonderful, Daniel. I had no idea you were so talented.'

'But——?' he prompted.

'But they seem to have been taken by somebody who's not at all like you. Or not like the way I perceive you.'

'And how exactly do you perceive me?'

There was a hostile edge to his voice, as if he was ready to cross swords with her. But, remembering the way he had taunted her about being a wimp, Beth did not retreat from the challenge.

'Ruthless, forceful, determined to have your own way,' she replied. 'And using every trick in the book to get it.'

'I'm flattered,' retorted Daniel sarcastically. 'And what exactly do these tricks consist of?'

'Charm,' said Beth. 'Physical attraction, a way with words. An ability to manipulate people, I suppose.'

Daniel glared at her with narrowed dark eyes. The air between them seemed to crackle with sudden antagonism.

'And supposing I tell you that I only ever use those tricks so people will do what's good for them?' he challenged.

Beth gave an impatient sigh.

'What difference does that make?' she demanded. 'What right do you have to play God and decide what's good for other people? Don't they have a right to make their own choices without undue pressure from you? Make their own mistakes, if necessary?'

He rose from the table and strode abruptly across the room with his hands dug deep in his pockets and a scowl on his face.

'Are we talking about you?' he asked, turning suddenly to face her. 'Is that what this is about? Are you regretting the fact that you agreed to work for me? Do you feel that I railroaded you into it?'

Beth let out a long sigh and toyed with the remains of a glass of white wine.

'No-o, I don't regret it exactly,' she admitted, draining the last dregs of the potent, slightly spritzing liquid. 'How could I? What's happening to me is so exciting and fulfilling. But I do worry sometimes about the way you talked me into it. You're so fluent with words that you just roll right over people.'

'I see,' retorted Daniel curtly.

He came striding back across the marble floor and crouched down suddenly beside her with one arm on her chair. He was so close that she could feel the warmth radiating out from his body, see the way his blue jeans stretched tautly over his muscular thighs, hear the rasp of his breathing. His dark eyes fixed her with glittering intensity.

'You're wrong about me,' he said in a tone of suppressed anger. 'I can see why you've got the idea that you have, but you're wrong. I was a Hollywood director for ten years and in that business you learn to hustle and flatter and second-guess people. But I'm not the kind of black-hearted villain you seem to think, Beth. I'd try to tell you what I really am and what I really want, but you'd probably say I was railroading you. So there's only one thing I can think of doing.'

Beth stared at him in bewilderment.

'What do you mean?' she demanded.

Daniel rose to his feet and stood gripping the back of one of the chairs as threateningly as if it were a deadly weapon.

'What I'm really good at, Beth, is getting an idea and making it real. A project, a movie, whatever. Translating dreams into life.'

Beth stared at him in perplexity.

Daniel strode about the room, clenching and unclenching his fists.

'Beth, did you ever see any of my movies?'

She shook her head, intrigued now.

'No.'

'Then will you watch one of them? That will give you a better idea of what kind of person I am than another two hours of talking.'

'All right,' agreed Beth slowly. 'I'd like to do that.'

She had expected to find the film entertaining, but what she was not prepared for was to be moved as profoundly as if some great crisis in her own life had overtaken her. Somehow she had been expecting a video, but Daniel pulled down a full-sized screen on one wall of the sitting-room and opened a teak cabinet to reveal a movie projector. When the lights went down and haunting guitar music flooded the room, Beth not only felt as if she had been transported into a cinema, she felt as if she had been transported back in time. The film was set in the eighteenth century and it was called *Alvaro's Choice*. It was the story of a young Spaniard studying for the priesthood in one of the Californian missions and the Chumash Indian girl whom he fell in

love with. Beth found it powerful, moving and profoundly disturbing.

If Daniel's aim was to convince her that he wasn't the
unfeeling tycoon that she believed, the film was certainly successful. But it also had an unexpected side-
effect. In the end what disturbed her most profoundly
was not just the powerful directing and photography but
the electrifying performance of Sunny Martino, who
played the part of the Indian girl. Probably by chance
the young Spanish actor who played the part of the priest
bore a slight physical resemblance to Daniel himself, and
in the scene where the pair became lovers, Beth found
herself so engrossed that she was sitting forward on her
seat.

Try as she might, she could not dismiss the uncanny
feeling that what she was watching was not a movie but
real life unfolding before her eyes. Sunny captured the
shyness, the humour and the innocence of the young
Indian girl so vividly that Beth found it almost unbearable to watch, particularly when she moved into the
arms of the hero. She realised that she had been cher-
ishing a comforting notion that Sunny Martino was
probably a hopeless actress who relied solely on her
physical charms. Reluctantly Beth now had to admit that
she was wrong. But just how wrong she did not realise
until the scene where Sunny found the Indian village reduced to ashes, her two children kidnapped and the body
of the man whom she believed to be Alvaro charred
beyond recognition. Her grief and frenzy was so over-
powering that Beth felt the hairs rising on the back of
her neck and her own throat so choked and tight she
could scarcely breathe. And in the final scene, when the
Indian girl came back to the beach where they had first
met and recognised Alvaro at the far end of the strand,
still alive and searching for her, Beth found tears running

openly down her face. As the two figures ran on a col-
lision course and the camera panned away from them
and up, up over the hills and out on to the ocean and
music soared and swirled around them and the credits
rolled on the screen, she rubbed her face surreptitiously
on her sleeve. By the time Daniel snapped on the light,
she had recovered enough to be blowing her nose vig-
orously and blinking her suspiciously red eyes.

'Well?' said Daniel, turning off the projector.

Beth hesitated, wondering how to put into words the
experience she had just had.

'It was magnificent,' she replied unsteadily. 'The love
story alone was really compelling and yet there was so
much more to it than that. The way they both ques-
tioned all the rules they had been brought up with. And
the way they were prepared to sacrifice anything to be
with each other and to do what they felt they must do.
I've never been so moved in my life by a film.'

Daniel smiled bleakly.

'Well, at least you understood what it was about,' he
said. 'Which was more than some of the critics did. What
did you think of Sunny?'

All Beth's senses seemed to be sharpened by her recent
contact with that haunting, lyrical movie. She could not
miss the note of pride and admiration and . . . love in
Daniel's voice. An unaccountable anger surged up inside
her, but she had to be honest.

'Sunny was superb,' she admitted and felt a tight ache
in her throat as if the words didn't want to come out.
'However did you get such a performance out of her?'

Daniel's angular, rather harsh features kindled.

'Sunny's a very special person,' he replied. 'She gave
me her whole heart and soul for that movie.'

In that moment Beth felt a pain as intense as if a knife
had stabbed into her. Suddenly she could no longer doubt

that Daniel was in love with Sunny Martino. Equally she could not doubt that she herself was far more dismayed by that than she should be. The image flashed into her mind of the burnt-out Indian village with its charred tent poles thrusting up against the wintry sky. An obscure feeling of misery settled on her.

'I think I'll go to bed now, if you'll excuse me,' she said stiffly. 'I'm rather tired.'

A momentary disappointment flashed in Daniel's eyes and then vanished.

'Just as you like,' he replied with apparent indifference.

There was no further mention of Sunny the following day and Daniel announced that he wanted to take Beth to Los Angeles. He was clearly in business-tycoon mode. Brisk, energetic and full of plans.

'I've already ordered a crew to put the barn into order at the farm at Buellton,' he started off. 'And pretty soon you'll have to start hiring staff to make up the clothes. The other thing you're going to need is a retail outlet in LA, and that's what we're checking out today. There's a store for lease on Rodeo Drive that I want you to take a look at.'

Beth gaped.

'Rodeo Drive?' she echoed. 'But isn't that hideously expensive? It's where the movie stars shop, isn't it?'

'Exactly,' agreed Daniel. 'And they're the customers you want. You're making a topline product, so you need a topline store to sell it.'

They arrived in Rodeo Drive just in time for lunch. There was a small pedestrian mall leading off to one side of the famous thoroughfare and it was here that the shop was situated which Daniel wanted her to inspect. But first he insisted that they eat at an outdoor café with huge shady white umbrellas and masses of white geraniums in terracotta tubs. After a feast of grilled lobster, salad, a cheese platter and fresh fruit, they went to look at the shop. It was in a three-storey building with an entranceway flanked by two tall graceful Ionian columns and a large plate-glass display area on the bottom floor. A tall black wrought-iron lampstand lent distinction to the pavement outside and there was the inevitable cluster of large terracotta pots containing red begonias and dwarf palm trees. The greenery was repeated on the balcony of the first floor with colourful red geraniums spilling downwards towards the street and white potato vines climbing the columns of the archway. Beth felt intimidated even looking at the place.

She felt even more intimidated when Daniel produced a set of keys from his pocket, unlocked the front door and led her inside. The building bore the unmistakable signs of wealth, from its luxurious velvety crimson carpet to the chandeliers overhead, the Regency-striped wallpaper and the large mahogany counter in one corner of the shop. A tour of the building showed that it had everything necessary for an upmarket fashion boutique. A delivery entrance at the rear, spacious changing cubicles, an office area, a kitchen and bathroom, racks of hanging space and a small staff tearoom. But Beth could not fight down her sense of misgiving, a feeling that she did not belong here, that she was an impostor. Her mind flashed back to the converted tool shed at the back of her parents' home where she had cut out her first dresses on a cement floor with mosquitoes whining around her legs. I don't belong here, she thought anxiously.

'What's wrong?' asked Daniel. He hoisted himself up lightly on to the mahogany counter and stared at her with a frown. 'You don't like the place. Why not?'

She gave a small, embarrassed shrug.

'I do like it,' she contradicted. 'But it's much too grand for me. Anyway I could never afford the rent.'

'Of course you can,' insisted Daniel contemptuously. 'I'll help you.'

Beth gave a long shuddering sigh.

'That's the problem,' she muttered.

'Come here,' growled Daniel, fixing her with his brooding dark eyes.

She hesitated, not wanting to obey him. And yet something about that unwinking stare mesmerised her so that she moved slowly towards him.

'Closer,' he said throatily.

She took a step closer and suddenly he closed his muscular thighs, trapping her between them. She started convulsively and made as if to back away, but he caught her by the shoulders.

'Don't be a fool,' he said roughly. 'You know I'm not going to hurt you. I just want to know the truth. What is it that's holding you back? Is it fear of failure or fear of what I'm going to ask of you?'

'Both,' she said.

His right hand came up and his fingers traced a warm, sensual line down the side of her cheek.

'You never fail until you give up trying,' he said. 'And I don't intend to ask anything of you except a business partnership. Yet.'

She shuddered. 'And later?' she asked.

'Later we'll see,' he said enigmatically. 'But don't let fear hold you back from spreading your wings, Beth. You have a lot of talent and you've got a duty to use it.'

With an unsteady gasp she broke away from him and paced across the room and then turning back she looked at him with a tormented expression.

'Why are you putting so much money and time into me?' she demanded. 'I know you said you're an entrepreneur, but do you do this for everyone whose business you back?'

'No, only the pretty ones,' said Daniel in a mocking voice.

Beth flinched.

'Oh, for heaven's sake!' Daniel burst out. 'It was a joke, Beth. OK, you can see perfectly well that I'm interested in you for more than just your talent as a fashion designer. I won't deny that. But I've told you before, my help with your business affairs is not conditional on your jumping into bed with me. *Is that clear*?'

His anger made her wince and it did little to soothe her fears. All right, maybe it was reassuring to know that Daniel wasn't going to demand any sexual favours in return for all his generosity, but he hadn't denied that he wanted her, either.

'Yes, it's clear,' she muttered. The words were agonisingly difficult to frame. 'But I still don't understand what you want from me.'

He slid off the counter with all the grace of a jungle cat and prowled across the room towards her. Then, catching her in his arms, he thrust his face down towards hers so close that she could feel his breath fanning her cheek and see the telltale beating of a pulse at his temple.

'When the time comes, sweetheart,' he said hoarsely, 'I'll leave you in no doubt at all about what I want. Until then, all I want to know is this: do you have the courage to gamble on your own talent or not?'

Beth shivered, conscious only of the tumultuously beating rhythm of her heart and the total insanity of letting this man sweep her away any further. She opened her mouth to protest, to refuse, to insist on struggling

back to safety while it was still possible, but somehow
her lips refused to frame the words.

'Y-yes,' she stammered, shocking herself deeply. 'Yes,
I do!'

For the next couple of weeks Daniel and Beth were
frantically busy in Los Angeles. There was the shop in
Rodeo Drive to be decorated and equipped, sales staff
to hire, fabric suppliers and agents to contact, and office
equipment to be bought. In addition Daniel insisted that
Beth spend five days at an intensive course on com-
puters and accounting and he took her on a tour of all
the leading fashion boutiques.

Their first weekend was spent working, but to Beth's
surprise on the second one Daniel announced that they
both deserved a holiday. Consequently they spent the
Saturday at Universal Studios being attacked by a deadly
twenty-foot shark and enduring all the thrills and horrors
of a runaway train, a laser battle with robots, an Alpine
avalanche, an encounter with King Kong and a dramatic
earthquake. Afterwards they had dinner in a shoji-
screened room at the Yamata restaurant. Savouring the
delights of shrimp *tempura* and green tea ice-cream, Beth
was surprised to find herself relaxing in simple, uncom-
plicated enjoyment. Unconsciously she had begun to feel
that her contact with Daniel had to consist of violent
confrontations or searingly passionate encounters. It was
surprising to find that he could also be a very good companion. Surprising and rather disturbing, because she
found herself wishing that this companionship would go
on.

The day after Beth finished her computer course,
Daniel announced abruptly that they were returning to
the horse farm in the Santa Ynez Valley.

'I've had the workmen in at your barn,' he said. 'So
I want to see how that's coming along. Besides, I'm

expecting delivery of a young thoroughbred filly and you're looking kind of tired. A break in the country would do you good.'

As they drove north from Los Angeles, Beth realised that she was tired. The three weeks since she had left Australia had vanished at a frantic pace and she could scarcely believe that so much had happened in such a short time. Her fashion collection had been lost and replaced, her business had taken off like a rocket and she had broken off her engagement to Warren. And all thanks to the ruthless and dynamic Daniel Pryor, a man who made her feel about as safe as if she were walking around the edge of a dormant volcano. Her face shadowed as she thought of how easily she had come to terms with the break-up with Warren. She had always believed that she loved him, so it was humiliating to feel that she could shrug him off so easily.

'What's wrong?' asked Daniel.

'I—I was thinking of Warren,' she blurted out.

He scowled ferociously.

'Well, don't,' he advised.

There was an uneasy silence between them for perhaps ten minutes until Daniel suddenly gestured to a beach on the left side of the road.

'That's the beach where we filmed part of *Alvaro's Choice*, down there,' he said.

Beth felt a sudden pang of jealousy at the image of Sunny Martino and the memory of Daniel's words. 'She gave me her whole heart and soul for that movie.' Gritting her teeth, she picked up a fashion magazine that was lying in her lap.

'That's nice,' she said coolly, opening it and turning the pages.

Daniel's mouth hardened, but he said nothing.

It was just after eleven o'clock when they reached the farm and the sun was blazing down out of a cloudless blue sky. Only a couple of weeks had elapsed since their previous visit, so Beth didn't expect much progress on the old barn which was to be her workplace. Consequently she was stunned when Daniel led her down to the building and flung open the main door.

'What do you think?' he asked.

She stepped inside and let out a low gasp. The place was transformed. In place of the sagging loose boxes, dirt floor and swags of cobwebs was a light, airy workroom with cutting benches, sewing machines, shelves for fabric storage and every imaginable item of equipment. Daniel led her through to the old tack-room and displayed an office painted in eggshell-blue with the old cedar fireplace meticulously restored and a discreet range of office furniture handcrafted in matching cedar. There was even a vase of flowers on Beth's desk next to the computer. Cornflowers. Beth walked over and touched them with disbelief written all over her face.

'Blue. To match your eyes,' said Daniel in a deadpan voice. 'I hope I've done it all the way you wanted.'

A lump rose in her throat and she stared at him with a feeling of misgiving. How could you cope with a man who anticipated your secret fantasies even before you had them yourself? A man who made dreams into reality with such relentless energy?

'Yes, you have. But how did you know what I would want?' she asked in perplexity. 'I didn't even know myself until now.'

Daniel shrugged.

'It wasn't difficult,' he replied with a touch of smugness. 'I asked Wendy Fulton for her advice on the practical equipment. As far as the décor went, I just tried to match it to the way I saw you. Efficient, conservative, but a romantic at heart.'

Beth stared at him with her lips parted and her heart thudding. It's unfair! she thought. No man on earth has a right to that kind of clairvoyance. Especially when he's as heartachingly gorgeous as Daniel Pryor. A tremulous warmth began to pulsate through her entire body and, as she stood mutely staring at Daniel, she knew how easy it would be simply to rush into his arms. Easy, but fatal. The image of her brother-in-law Greg flashed into her mind and alarm bells rang. Daniel was standing there with his hands on his hips, surveying her out of half-closed eyes with just the same mocking, inviting smile she had once found so irresistible in Greg. The memory made her go cold and rigid with dismay.

'It's very nice,' she said stiffly. 'Exactly what I wanted. Thank you so much.'

Daniel looked at her calmly. 'No transports of delight, huh? OK, Beth, we'll play it your way. But one of these days I'll find out how to get through that cool façade to the real woman underneath. And that's a promise.'

CHAPTER EIGHT

'WHERE are you going?' cried Beth.

'Back to the barn,' he said over his shoulder. 'I want to see if my filly has arrived.'

He hurried away with such long, furious strides that Beth couldn't have kept up with him if she had wanted to. And she wasn't at all sure that she did. For some reason she had lost the urge to quarrel with him. Suddenly she felt mean, hateful, a spoilsport. It was obvious that Daniel had been looking forward to giving her a wonderful surprise and she had spoilt it all by the coldness of her reaction. Why did she have to worry so much about whether he was trying to seduce her? Couldn't she just relax and go with the flow instead of trying to keep herself safe all the time? Remorsefully she hurried after him to apologise. He was just coming out of the main barn when she caught him up and laid her hand on his arm.

'I'm sorry, Daniel,' she said impulsively. 'I'm thrilled with the barn. Honestly, I am. And I didn't mean to hurt your feelings.'

He looked at her with a brooding expression for a moment longer, then a faint smile touched the corners of his mouth.

'No harm done,' he assured her. 'And Eric says my filly won't be here for a couple of hours. So how about coming for a trail ride with me up into the hills? We could take a picnic.'

Beth's eyes widened.

'I'd love it,' she agreed. 'But I should warn you I've never been on a horse in my life before.'

Daniel gave a low growl of laughter.

'In that case I'll find you a walking armchair,' he promised.

The trail ride was fun although Beth was alarmed to discover that the horse's back seemed much narrower once she was actually sitting on it. But the bay mare was friendly, and did nothing but shake her bridle and snort resignedly when Daniel hoisted Beth aboard. He showed her how to hold the reins correctly and to set her feet so that only her toes were in the stirrups and then they headed off down a trail overhung by eucalyptus trees and glossy red Chinese fire bushes which had escaped from the garden. Now and then Beth caught a glimpse of the blue hills high above them but most of the time she was content to concentrate on staying in the saddle. It was pleasant to feel the hot sun beating down on her back and to smell the mingled aromas of dry grass, leather and horseflesh. There was no sound but the creak of the saddles, the shrilling of insects in the dry grass and once the lazy drone of a light aircraft overhead. Bit by bit Beth felt herself begin to relax. At last they came out in a sunny clearing on top of the hill.

'Well, this is it,' said Daniel, dismounting. 'My favourite picnic spot.'

He flung the reins over his horse's head and came across to help Beth. As she stepped down on to firm ground she had the sudden unnerving sensation that her legs were made of rubber, and had to clutch at the stirrup leathers.

'Oops,' she said. 'My bones seem to have vanished.'

Daniel grinned.

'You'll get used to it,' he assured her. 'But since it's your first ride I'll take pity on you and get the lunch ready myself. Just a minute and I'll fix you a place to sit.'

Deftly he unsaddled the horses and spread the saddle blankets on the ground, motioning Beth to sit down. She rolled her eyes in surprise but obeyed. The blankets smelled strongly of horse and yet it was rather pleasant to be sitting there on the sunlit grass, leaning against an ornate Western saddle and watching Daniel unpack various small packages of food. Before long he had a simple but appetising meal prepared. Crusty French bread, butter, ham, crisp red apples and a bottle of white wine.

'I'd like to know what you think of the wine,' he said, pouring her some in an acrylic glass. 'It comes from a vineyard in the Napa Valley that's one of my pet projects.'

Beth sipped cautiously, appreciating the light fruity bouquet.

'It tastes great to me,' she said. 'Although I'm no expert. But whatever made you get involved with a vineyard?'

Daniel shrugged.

'Well, the young couple who make this came to me and asked for a loan,' he said. 'On the face of it it didn't look too promising. They'd been in business before and a fire had wiped out their entire stock and their insurance just wasn't adequate to cover the damage. But they knew what they wanted and they wanted it very badly. They'd done their homework and they were prepared to work hard. I couldn't ask any more than that, so I gave them the loan they needed. That was five years ago.'

'And now?' asked Beth.

'And now they're doing very nicely,' said Daniel. A smile touched the corners of his mouth. 'And so am I. I've been lucky in my investments.'

'Or shrewd,' suggested Beth.

'Or shrewd,' he agreed, without any false modesty.

'What made you buy this place?' asked Beth, gesturing at the valley below.

Daniel grinned ruefully.

'Mainly the fact that I wanted to be a cowboy when I was a kid,' he said. 'I found Boston stifling. And even when I grew up I felt the same way. Three-piece suits and boardrooms and cocktail parties just aren't my style. I like to be outdoors.'

'So do you spend much time here?' enquired Beth lazily. She was finding it rather difficult to butter French bread lying down, but felt too rubber-legged to get up.

'Not as much as I'd like,' replied Daniel, plucking a piece of grass and chewing it. 'Although I have been here more often in the last year or so since I gave up directing movies.'

'Why did you give up?' asked Beth. 'You were awfully good at it.'

'Thank you,' said Daniel, throwing away his piece of grass and reaching for a plate. 'Pass me the ham, will you? Now, where were we? Why did I give up the movies? Several reasons. I got tired of the rat race, getting up before dawn, fighting the freeways, constantly hustling people. And I'd made more money than was decent. So I decided I'd use some of it to help other people achieve their dreams.'

Beth flashed him a startled look. 'That's very noble of you!' she exclaimed.

'Noble? Hell, no! It's been fun,' protested Daniel. 'I wouldn't have done it otherwise.'

'So what kind of dreams have you put into action?' she asked.

Daniel smiled reminiscently.

'Let me see. A candy store in Solvang, run by a paraplegic girl with the face of an angel and the brain of a Swiss banker. The Napa Valley vineyard, a computer software firm, a boatyard in the San Francisco Bay area. And about twenty others, including yours.'

Beth shifted uneasily, somehow resenting the way Daniel lumped her in with the rest. I want to be special to him, she thought. And then, looking at his muscular body stretched lazily beside her, realised what a dangerous ambition that was. He reminded her of some jungle cat lazing here in the golden sunlight, apparently drowsy and harmless, but full of potential menace. Something about the way his eyes narrowed and his tongue rubbed along his lower lip made every nerve in her body quiver with alarm. Hastily she sought to change the subject.

'So will you ever make another movie?' she asked.

'Probably not.'

'Not even that sequel you said you were going to do?'

'What sequel?'

'I don't know. To something called *Destiny's Favourite*. You told the reporters at the fashion parade in LA that you were thinking of doing it.'

Daniel threw back his head with a sudden rumble of laughter. Then he whistled a few bars of a haunting little melody.

'Oh, that? No! *Destiny's Favourite* was a television soapie that gave Sunny and me our start years ago. It was really popular and people are always clamouring for another series, but I don't have any serious intention of making one. That was just a bit of timely fantasy to throw the reporters off the scent.'

'Why did you do that?' asked Beth.

'Well, good old Warren was obviously hell-bent on telling them all about our boating accident,' said Daniel with a touch of bitterness. 'I didn't want every detail of my first meeting with you splashed all over the glossy papers. Did you?'

To her surprise, he trailed his finger slowly down the inside of her arm. Beth flinched and looked up at him to see that his eyes were fixed on hers with smouldering intensity. Her heart began to beat faster and for some reason she had difficulty breathing. Why would Daniel care so much about gossip writers discussing their first meeting unless...? She left the thought unfinished and looked hastily away.

'No,' she said in a high, unnatural voice, aware that her cheeks were flushing. 'It must be awful to have your private life on display like that. I'm glad you stopped Warren.'

Coolly, almost insolently, Daniel seized her chin and turned her face back to his so that she could not avoid looking at him.

'Speaking of Warren, what is happening between you two now?'

Beth's heart was beating so frantically that she felt it would leap out of her chest. A helpless tide of longing swept through her, making her feel weak and shaky. Daniel was gazing down at her so intently and tilting her chin with such passionate urgency that she knew at any moment he would kiss her. And not just a butterfly brush on the lips, either. If she revealed that she had broken off with Warren permanently, what would Daniel do?

A fierce, throbbing warmth spreading through every part of her body warned her all too clearly of what she would like him to do. Desperately she took in a long, uneven breath.

'Oh, nothing's changed,' she babbled brightly. 'Warren's still in New York right now, but of course when he gets back, he'll come straight to see me.'

'Of course,' sneered Daniel, releasing her chin with a jerk. 'You're still too much of a fool to see that he doesn't really love you and that he isn't going to marry you. But I can see it a mile off.'

Beth scrambled to her feet, feeling suddenly that a rug in a sunlit clearing was not the safest place to be when Daniel Pryor was crouching beside her with that sort of expression on his face.

'Oh, so you're the expert on love and marriage, are you?' she demanded in a voice that was meant to be cool, but sounded unexpectedly ragged.

Like a panther springing into action, Daniel too rose to his feet. Her height gave her no advantage, for he towered a good six inches above her and was lean and hard and muscular to match. His fingers closed around her arm like a handcuff.

'Why shouldn't I be?' he snarled.

'Have you ever been in love?' she challenged.

His eyes were like dark, smouldering beacons.

'Once,' he agreed hoarsely. 'When I was young and as gullible as you are.'

'And did you marry?'

'No. She wouldn't have me.'

A succession of emotions flitted across his face. Pain. Anger. Contempt. Indifference. Beth felt a flare of jealousy towards that unknown woman who had rejected Daniel. Why had he loved her and why didn't she care for him? Even worse, the momentary hurt in Daniel's eyes sent a twinge of sympathy shooting through Beth. She felt a dangerous urge to take him in her arms and comfort him. Ruthlessly she suppressed it.

'So that makes you an expert on everyone else's love-affairs, does it?' she demanded sarcastically.

A stormy expression blazed in his eyes.

'I learnt a thing or two, yes.'

'Enough to tell me what I should be doing, I suppose?'

With a sudden, ruthless movement he crushed her against him, holding her so hard that she could feel his warm, aroused maleness against her.

'I could not only tell you what you should be doing. I could show you,' he said hoarsely. 'But I'm not going to do it. You accused me once already of manipulation and I've had a gutful of this pretence that I'm hustling you in a direction you don't want to take. When you come to me, sweetheart, you'll do it willingly. From here on in, if you want me, you'll have to make the next move. Now let's get the horses saddled. We're leaving.'

On the way back down Beth brooded over the things Daniel had said. She felt hurt and angry about his accusations, although she also had to admit there was a kernel of truth in them. He was right about the way she kept pretending she didn't want him, when in reality her whole body was on fire with longing for him. Yet what else could she do? She didn't want to rebound from one disastrous relationship into another and she really didn't know enough yet to trust him, although she had certainly learnt more today. For once he had let some of his habitual wariness slip, and for the first time she had glimpsed the vulnerability of the man beneath that confident, arrogant exterior. But his revelations were tantalisingly incomplete. Was Sunny Martino the woman he loved? And why did he keep seeing her if she wouldn't marry him? And why on earth should Beth care? With a determined effort she pushed the whole disastrous subject out of her mind and tried to enjoy the rest of the ride.

When they reached the barn a horse-box was already drawn up outside and Daniel, with a curt apology to Beth, helped her dismount and then handed over both horses to Eric before vanishing into the barn. Eric smothered a grin as Beth hobbled across the driveway.

'Jenny has just made some fresh coffee if you'd like some,' he advised. 'And she might have some liniment for the sore spots too.'

'It'll need more than liniment,' muttered Beth. 'It'll need major surgery.' But she made her way along under the loggia to knock on Jenny's kitchen door.

'Hi, come in,' said Jenny, pushing open the screen door. 'Where's Daniel?'

'In the barn with the new filly,' replied Beth. 'And I'd kill for a cup of coffee.'

Jenny smiled, rolling her eyes in mock alarm.

'No need for that,' she assured her. 'How do you like it?'

'With milk, please. No sugar.'

The coffee was strong, hot and reviving. To accompany it Jenny produced a plate of small, ball-shaped doughnuts dusted with powdered sugar and served with raspberry jam.

'Try my *Aebleskiver*,' she urged. 'They're a local delicacy.'

'Mmm, delicious,' said Beth appreciatively. 'Have you known Daniel long, Jenny?'

She told herself that she was only making conversation, but she knew that there was more to it than that. The truth was that she was hungry for every crumb of information she could get about Daniel. Jenny's eyes took on a far-away look and her lips moved as if she were calculating.

'About twelve years,' she agreed. 'Eric and I handled the horses for him on some of his early movies. Then when he bought this place he offered us a job here.'

'What's he like to work for?' asked Beth casually.

Jenny's eyebrows shot up.

'Unpredictable,' she replied. 'Infuriating. A lot of fun. All those things and more. Daniel's a strange guy. In some ways he really brings out the best in people. He gets you to do things you'd never believe you were capable of. But he's maddeningly aloof about himself. You never really know what he's thinking or what he's planning because he doesn't give much away. And he likes to be in control of things, to feel that he's the boss and he's directing what's happening. Mind you, that often works very well. He's made some wonderful movies. Have you seen any of them?'

'I saw *Alvaro's Choice*,' agreed Beth.

'What did you think of it?'

Beth sighed.

'It was brilliant,' she admitted. 'The cinematography was superb, the directing was amazingly raw and powerful and I have to admit that Sunny Martino acted magnificently in it.'

'You have to admit,' echoed Jenny thoughtfully. 'Don't you like Sunny, then?'

Beth flushed. 'I'm not sure,' she said. 'I've only met her once.'

Jenny looked at her keenly.

'Well, she's a pretty tough cookie,' she admitted. 'And Daniel is certainly very attached to her.'

'Is he?' asked Beth too quickly.

Jenny's eyes met hers. An uncomfortable expression spread over her face. She pleated the edge of the table-cloth between her fingers and looked down.

'Look, I may be right out of line in saying this, Beth, but be careful with Daniel, won't you? I don't quite know what the situation is between you two, but I wouldn't like to see you get hurt. Daniel's a pretty dynamic guy, with a lot of women running after him, but the only one I've ever seen last for any length of time is Sunny Martino.'

Beth felt a heavy painful feeling in her throat as if she had just swallowed a large stone.

'Are they lovers?' she asked awkwardly.

Jenny gave her a worried look.

'Most people seem to think so,' she said. 'I honestly don't know for sure, but I think it's likely. There's a rumour that Sunny is secretly married to somebody else, but personally I doubt it. But I do know she comes up here quite often and she always stays at Daniel's house. What goes on between them I have no idea. But just...be careful, Beth. OK?'

'OK,' agreed Beth hoarsely.

At that moment the wire door of the kitchen opened and Daniel appeared. Both women started guiltily and Beth wondered whether Daniel had overheard their conversation but there was nothing in the least self-conscious about his manner when he spoke.

'I've got the filly in one of the loose boxes now, Beth,' he said. 'I thought you might like to come and see her get started up.'

Beth blinked.

'Started up?' she echoed in bafflement. 'What does that mean?'

'It's a term used by one of the finest horse trainers in the world,' he explained, 'who just happens to live in this valley. He doesn't like to talk about breaking in horses because it sounds as if you're breaking their spirit. This is a method of persuading a horse to accept a rider which is based totally on trust, not fear. No force is ever used and the animal itself makes the choice to accept the rider.'

'All right. That sounds interesting,' agreed Beth. 'I'd like to see it.'

'Come on, then.'

Daniel led her outside to the training pen. This was a large circular structure about fifty feet in diameter with a solid wall about eight feet high and a roof. Taking Beth's hand, he showed her up a ramp to an observation deck.

'Now this is something really worth seeing,' he told her. 'We've got a two-year-old thoroughbred filly who is completely unbroken but half an hour from now I'm going to have a saddle on her back and ride her around here.'

'In half an hour?' echoed Beth. 'That's impossible!'

'Just watch,' said Daniel. 'Once I gain her trust, anything is possible.'

He touched Beth's cheek lightly and then strode away down the ramp. Five minutes later Daniel led the horse into the ring. Beth let out a soft sigh of admiration at the sight of the beautiful animal standing still in a shaft of sunlight. The filly was about fifteen hands high, a dark bay in colour, with a white blaze on her forehead, and she was obviously very, very nervous. Her head tossed restlessly against the halter, her eyes rolled showing the whites and she stamped her feet, letting out nervous, protesting whinnies. But Daniel calmly led her into the centre of the pen and introduced himself by rubbing his hand around the horse's forehead. After a while, when she seemed to accept him, he moved around to the rear of her and, standing clear of any possible kicks, suddenly pitched a long line towards her rear quarters.

With a flurry of panic the filly took flight and cantered round and round the pen, but Daniel followed her, pursuing her in circles and keeping up the same movement with the line. The exhausting flight continued, but after a while Daniel positioned himself so that the animal had to turn and go in the opposite direction. It was at this point that Beth began to watch with total absorption. Some silent dialogue seemed to be going on between Daniel and the animal. She saw him watching closely and followed his gaze, but could see nothing herself except that one of the animal's ears seemed to stay still while the other one twitched. Bit by bit the filly's head began to tip and her neck bent. Slowly Daniel coiled the line and stood with his eyes down. Holding her breath, Beth saw the animal take a hesitant step towards him, then another, then stop still, uncertainly looking at Daniel. The silence lengthened and Beth became acutely conscious of the motes of dust dancing in the sunlight, the smell of horse sweat and the animal's soft, whickering breath. Picking its way delicately across the ring, the horse suddenly butted the man playfully in the chest. Beth was so moved that she had to swallow hard as she watched Daniel affectionately rubbing the filly's forehead. Looking down at her watch, she could scarcely believe that no more than four minutes had passed since they first entered the ring.

From here on everything seemed easy. Before long the filly was following Daniel around the pen. From time to time he stopped and rubbed her affectionately all over her back and legs, and when the bond between them seemed to be firmly established he brought in a saddle and bridle and allowed her to look it over. Then in easy stages he persuaded the filly to let him put the unfamiliar equipment on her back. The only frightening moment for Beth was when Daniel at last flung himself into the saddle. After a moment's outraged paralysis the horse bucked fiercely all the way around the ring. But Daniel simply laughed and patted her neck. At the end of the half-hour, just as he had promised, he was riding the horse serenely around the pen and it was clear that a warm bond of affection had developed between them. At this point he raised his hand in a brief salute to Beth and walked the animal quietly away.

'Well, what did you think of it?' he asked when he returned five minutes later.

Beth stared at him, taking in every detail of his broad powerful shoulders, the dark hair visible through his open-necked check shirt, the way his jeans clung to his muscular thighs. Taking in also the warmth and sense of achievement that glowed in his dark eyes. She thought of the gentleness and patience Daniel had shown in dealing with the nervous filly and felt a whimsical pang of sympathy with the animal. Like the thoroughbred horse, Beth both yearned and feared to trust him. But a man who could show such affection to a dumb animal must be good at heart. Mustn't he?

'I thought it was wonderful,' she said honestly. 'It was one of the most moving experiences I've ever had in my life.'

Daniel's lean brown fingers reached out and touched her cheek.

'Good,' he murmured. He made a slight movement towards her and for a moment she thought he was going to kiss her. She felt her lips part in anticipation, but he simply touched her on the shoulder and moved past her towards the house. She followed after him with a turbulent feeling of regret. Jenny's warning rang in her ears. 'Don't fall in love with him.' But she knew it was too late. For better or worse, she already had.

CHAPTER NINE

THE realisation that she was in love with Daniel threw Beth into a tailspin of panic. A few minutes' quiet reflection soon convinced her of one thing. The mere fact that Daniel was kind to animals didn't necessarily mean that he was trustworthy when it came to people. If she had any sense, she would ruthlessly crush these emotions before they raged totally out of control. It had been bad enough when she had only felt disturbingly attracted to him. But to have lost her heart to him was sheer madness. Worse still, it was a madness that showed no sign of abating.

Fortunately the Kronborgs invited them both to dinner and there was enough noise, laughter and confusion at the table for Beth's quietness to pass unremarked. With Jake holding forth about body-building, Candice trying to wheedle money for a rock concert and Amy spilling stew in her lap, Beth could sit unnoticed. A fate for which she was silently grateful. The aroma of beef and jacket potatoes, the lamplight winking off the silver, the buzz of conversation all blurred into a dim and unimportant background as she sat watching Daniel with a kind of desperate yearning.

No, he wasn't really good-looking at all, she decided. His eyebrows were too fierce, his nose too powerful, his jaw too aggressive. And even if the sight of his muscular brown arms upraised in an emphatic argument with Eric did cause a strange fluttering deep inside her, she knew it was foolish. Just a quiet, crazy disturbance in her usual calm good sense, not worth worrying about. Perhaps the best thing to do was to let this odd obsession take its course and then it wouldn't bother her any more. Maybe if she just looked at him as much as she liked and let her tantalising fantasies flow freely, she would get over it all much faster. Resting her chin on her hands, she gazed mistily at him, wondering what it would be like to run her hands down the taut, flat muscles of his belly...

'Is something wrong, Beth?'

His voice jarred her back to reality. Colour washed through her face and her heart thudded fiercely. It doesn't work! she thought in torment. It only makes it worse and, oh, help, he knows...

'N-no, nothing!' she stammered.

Their eyes met and held. A flickering, provocative smile hovered around the edges of Daniel's mouth and the room seemed to spin away. All that remained was the shrewd, knowing look on Daniel's face and the unsteady hammering of Beth's heart. She wanted to leap to her feet and flee, but was held captive by the chains of good manners, normality, the need to pretend that nothing was happening. Nothing at all.

'I thought I'd drive back to LA tomorrow,' announced Daniel, his eyes still boring into her, still full of questions, 'start setting up the shop on Rodeo Drive. You can come with me if you like. Unless you'd rather stay here and get started on the production end of the business?'

'No... Yes... I—I would,' replied Beth disjointedly. 'Rather stay here I mean.'

The intolerable nature of her predicament was just beginning to sink in. What she really wanted to do at this moment was to vanish through the floor. Or, failing that, race out of the room and catch a plane back to Australia where with luck she would never make such a fool of herself again. But the fact was that she was trapped. Daniel had spent countless thousands of dollars on refurbishing the barn and leasing the shop in Los Angeles. She couldn't leave now, just because of the ridiculous and embarrassing fact that she had fallen in love with him. All she could do was try and pretend it hadn't happened.

'No, I'd rather stay here,' she repeated. And this time, to her relief, it was her business voice that spoke. Cool, crisp, controlled. 'I've got heaps of work to do and I'll probably manage better on my own.'

It was true in a way. She did manage better on her own than if Daniel had been there to torment her with his brooding dark eyes, the touch of his strong hands, the careless grace of his movements. Well, at least in the daytime she managed better, when she could spend twelve or fourteen hours at a stretch drawing and cutting and planning and telephoning. Hasty discussions with Wendy, long sessions pacing the workroom floor to check the progress of the garments, endless hassles with fabric supplies and tradesmen—these all helped to dull the longing for Daniel.

But at night it was a different matter. When she withdrew to her cottage at eight or nine o'clock, it was still too early to sleep. Sometimes she filled the lonely hours writing letters to her mother about her new life. Sometimes she thought about Warren, but Warren seemed curiously remote and unimportant. Most of the time she ended up doing exactly what she had dreaded— mooning around thinking about Daniel. One night she lay on her bed and made a list of all the things she knew about him, but the facts seemed curiously lifeless. Thirty-six years old, born and raised in Boston, only child of divorced parents, former film producer and director, current business entrepreneur, dark-haired, dark-eyed, unmarried. Yet the list didn't capture the extraordinary magnetism and vitality that was so typical of Daniel, the way the air in a room seemed to become electrically charged when he walked in. It didn't explain why he was so tempestuously attractive to women, but had never married. And it didn't tell Beth whether his interest in her was simply a sexual game or the first turbulent sign of an answering love. The uncertainty tormented her so badly that in the end she did what she had sworn she wouldn't do. She telephoned his apartment in Los Angeles. A woman's voice answered. Sunny Martino's voice. Beth felt as if she had been struck in the face.

'Is Daniel there, please?' she asked, wondering if the tightness in her throat meant that she was catching the flu.

'I'll get him,' replied Sunny.

Was it Beth's imagination or did the actress's voice sound just as taut and unfriendly as her own?

Daniel came on the line and Beth sat as if she were paralysed. Overjoyed to hear his voice and yet hating him, because he had Sunny there at ten-thirty at night and not her. Why? What were they doing? Did she even want to know?

'Beth? Is something wrong?' The sharp note of concern in his voice made her feel guilty and foolish.

'No... I just wanted to talk to you... That is, yes. I have a problem with Customs about the wool and fabric imports from Australia.'

She went on talking haltingly, agonisingly, wondering if she ought to just slam down the phone and never speak to him again.

'How about if I drive up tomorrow and sort this out?' he cut in. 'That would be best. I'll take you to lunch in Solvang.'

Solvang was a delight. Picture-postcard pretty with Danish windmills and flower boxes of red geraniums, yellow marigolds and blue lobelias. They ate in an outdoor restaurant at a table with a shady umbrella and a pretty blonde waitress in a white lace blouse and some kind of dirndl pinafore frisked around with plates of Danish delicacies. But Beth didn't taste a bite of it. Not a bite. Because she was so busy devouring Daniel with her eyes and wishing savagely that he hadn't come or that she knew where on earth she stood with him. I love him, she thought angrily. But there's no future in it.

As she sat pushing a wedge of fresh cantaloupe melon around her plate Daniel suddenly surprised her by leaning forward and trailing his finger down the inside of her wrist.

'Did you miss me?' he asked abruptly.

She gave him a startled look and for a moment she was on the brink of blurting out just how much she had missed him and why, and then she remembered Sunny in his apartment at night and her mouth hardened.

'Don't be silly,' she said lightly. 'You've only been gone for a few days. Why should I have missed you?'

He shrugged.

'No reason,' he admitted. Then he leaned towards her and his voice dropped to a deep, soft burr too low to be heard by anyone else. 'Except that we did agree that from here on you'd make the next move. I thought perhaps this was it.'

'Don't be ridiculous,' said Beth sharply. 'I only phoned you because I wanted to discuss my problems with Customs.'

'All right,' agreed Daniel with a sigh. 'If that's what you want.'

With his usual efficiency he had disposed of her query within two minutes, but to her relief he showed no sign of returning to their earlier conversation. Instead he poured himself another glass of Danish beer and raised it to her in a brief salute.

'Your designs did well at the trade show in New York,' he said. 'Congratulations. I suppose you've heard all about it by now?'

'Yes, I have,' agreed Beth. And perhaps because his intense scrutinising gaze made her feel so uncomfortable she was tempted to add, 'Warren phoned and told me.'

It wasn't true, but Daniel didn't know that.

'You're still seeing him then?' he demanded.

'Yes,' lied Beth.

'Then you're a bigger fool than I took you for,' said Daniel contemptuously.

Beth was already beginning to regret the malicious impulse that had prompted her statement, so she hastily changed the subject.

'How's the shop on Rodeo Drive coming along?' she asked. The hostile anger still lurked in Daniel's dark eyes, but he replied civilly enough.

'Fine. I think we should be ready for the grand opening on Monday week if that suits you.'

Beth nodded.

'Yes, it will,' she agreed. 'Wendy and the girls have been working like demons. We'll have plenty of stock to put on the racks.'

'Good,' agreed Daniel briskly. 'Then I'll organise everything at the LA end. I thought maybe a fashion parade out in the mall with a string quartet, champagne, hors-d'oeuvres, a few well-known actors and actresses to kick things off.'

'Like Sunny Martino, I suppose,' suggested Beth tartly.

Daniel looked at her thoughtfully.

'Now why the acid note in your voice when you mention Sunny?' he challenged. 'Yes, as a matter of fact

I do think Sunny would help our cause and she is willing to come along and spend money and be photographed. Besides, she asked me to pass on an invitation to you.'

'An invitation?' said Beth swiftly. 'What kind of invitation?'

'She wants to host a small dinner party after the opening. Only eight or ten people. She says she'd like to get to know you better. Will you come?'

Beth stared at him in dismay. An unpleasant feeling of confusion swept over her. She should have been grateful for Sunny's offer and would have been if it had not been for her connection to Daniel. As it was she felt miserably reluctant to be under an obligation to the actress.

'Do I have to?' she protested.

Daniel sighed impatiently.

'She's doing you a favour, Beth,' he snapped. 'Having Sunny Martino wear your designs and publicise them will do wonders for your career. And what's more Sunny is one of my oldest and dearest friends. I'm not going to give you any orders, since you seem to have some kind of weird objection to my doing that. But yes, I want you to be there.'

The ordeal was every bit as bad as Beth had feared. Oh, the opening of the shop on Rodeo Drive went well enough. In fact it was just like a miniature repetition of the performance at the Cadogan Hall fashion show. Clients and spectators thronged the pedestrian mall, a string quartet played light music, beautiful models paraded up and down the outdoor catwalk, gallons of champagne were drunk and the cash register rang merrily for a couple of hours. But the really hard part began when they all returned to Sunny's house in Beverly Hills. It was a strange structure of grey stucco that looked as if it had been made out of children's building blocks.

Two huge windows shaped like Thermos flasks projected from the front wall and there were four identical white garages below them. Sunny parked her Jaguar in one of these and then urged her guests up the stairway to one side of the house. Beth had met them all at the opening at Rodeo Drive, but had forgotten half their names. So it was rather a relief when Sunny repeated the introductions once they were inside the spacious entrance hall.

'All right, now,' she cried with a shrill squeal of laughter. 'Do you all know who you are? Well, I guess you guys all know each other but Beth probably doesn't remember so, left to right, me, Sunny; Daniel; Beth; Lane Galloway; Alice Hutchinson; Nick Weinberg; Leonie Cleaver and Scott Barrett. Right, now let's go get ourselves a drink.'

She shooed them all into a living-room which was so brightly coloured it made Beth feel quite bilious. Light poured down from a mezzanine gallery overhead revealing a collection of furniture that was alarmingly futuristic. Over by one wall was a red padded couch which looked as though it had started out life as a weight-lifting bench or surgical trolley. In the centre of the room was a day-bed brightly upholstered in yellow and blue and sitting on a base of grey laminated material. A glass trolley with backward-tilted legs held a collection of objects that looked like spare parts from a motorcycle, but which proved on closer inspection to be a modern teapot and cups. On the far wall was a huge abstract painting in swirls of magenta and bright green and in front of the large bay window was a brightly coloured geometrical piece of furniture which Beth thought was probably a bookcase. The floor was made of hard black slate.

'Well, make yourselves comfortable,' urged Sunny optimistically. 'And let's get some drinks.'

She pressed something which looked like a piece of abstract sculpture and a loud buzzer sounded through the house. Moments later there was the sound of soft footsteps.

'You rang, madam?'

'Benson!' cried Beth.

It was the English butler who had been aboard Daniel's yacht at their first meeting. Beth had met him several times since then and they had struck up quite a friendship, based on a mutual interest in cooking. Finding him here tonight was like meeting a secret ally.

'Indeed, madam,' agreed Benson with a faint smile. 'It's good to see you again.'

While Benson was taking their orders for drinks, Beth sat down on the brightly coloured day-bed in the centre of the room and tried to get her bearings. Her initial pleasure at seeing Benson was beginning to evaporate as she wondered what on earth he was doing here. Didn't it show a fairly intense level of intimacy between Sunny and Daniel if the butler flitted between one household and the other?

A sudden shriek of laughter from across the room caught Beth's attention and she looked up. Sunny was evidently telling jokes to Daniel and had just collapsed with amusement all over his shoulder. Beth's lips twisted at the spectacle. Not half so intense as the level of intimacy she's reaching now, she thought coldly.

'Gin and tonic, Beth?'

A tall, handsome man with brown curly hair was bearing down on her. He gave her a stunning smile and sat down beside her.

'Thank you,' she said.

'I'm Lane Galloway,' he explained. 'I act in the soaps. And I hear you're going great guns with this new fashion design business. Tell me all about it.'

Hesitantly Beth began to talk, but her mind wasn't really on the conversation. She kept darting swift glances at Daniel and Sunny over on the surgical trolley. Sunny had slipped off her red satin jacket and her dramatic bustline was bouncing merrily with every gasp of laughter. Lane Galloway too seemed to be riveted by the sight.

'Sorry?' he said suddenly. 'What were you saying?'

Beth sighed. 'You don't have to sit and entertain me, you know,' she replied frankly. 'It's kind of you, but I'll be fine on my own.'

'Oh, that's OK,' insisted the actor. 'I'm happy to do it. Besides, Sunny asked me to.'

That naïve remark made Beth's cheeks burn and her brain work furiously. Why would Sunny ask another man to dance attendance on Beth? To keep her away from Daniel, of course! By the time they sat down to dinner, Beth was simmering with annoyance.

The meal itself was excellent. Seafood brochettes followed by seasoned pheasant with wild rice and green salad, and chocolate strawberries in toffee baskets accompanied by the best Californian wine. But Beth found the byplay among the guests nerve-racking in the extreme. The others were an oddly assorted group of people, obviously chosen for the purpose of helping to launch Beth's designs. Alice was a gossip columnist, Nick a photographer, Scott a marketing manager and Leonie was Beth's agent. Before long they were all deep in discussion about the best strategy for making Solo Designs a runaway hit. Beth knew she should have been grateful, but somehow she wasn't. A lot of Sunny's ideas were good. Very good. She had just suggested holding a

charity auction of the wedding-dress from Beth's up-
coming winter collection and she was now in full spate
about getting photos taken in British Columbia to advertise the cold-weather gear. Yet Beth found it impossible to join in the spirit of things. She hated the way
Sunny kept throwing Daniel sly, intimate looks and
asking his opinion on everything. And what annoyed
her even more was the way Daniel refused to meet her
eye. Whenever Beth looked at him, he simply gave a
bored smile and returned immediately to watching Sunny.

Once the coffee and port were finished Beth made her
escape with relief to the huge bedroom which Sunny had
set aside as a cloakroom for the women guests. She was
waiting her turn to use the bathroom when Sunny joined
her. Beth gave her a frozen smile.

'Thank you for the meal,' she said stiffly. 'It was
delicious.'

Sunny didn't give one of her shrill squeals of laughter.
Instead she smiled soberly and put her hand on Beth's
arm.

'Don't be uptight about all this, Beth,' she urged.
'Once the business party leaves and there's only Lane
and Daniel and us, we'll get along fine. You'll see.'

At that moment Alice emerged from the bathroom
and Sunny gave Beth a warning look. For a moment she
wondered what on earth the actress meant and then
shrugged. It was obvious, wasn't it? Once everyone else
had left, Lane Galloway would obediently fawn all over
Beth, leaving Sunny free to grapple with Daniel. The
prospect filled Beth with a leaden sense of dismay.

When she came out to rejoin the others five minutes
later, this scenario already seemed to be well under way.
Sunny, wearing a dramatic red brocade evening dress
with cornelli trim, which Beth herself had designed, was
posing for photos with Daniel. Beth sat down on a couch

and watched with a sense of smouldering resentment as the actress draped herself slinkily all over him. For an instant Daniel's eyes flickered to meet hers, then he looked back at Nick's camera and smiled blandly. Lane Galloway suddenly appeared on the couch beside her.

'Don't take this too seriously,' he muttered under his breath. 'It's just showbiz. Hey, how about a glass of port?'

Beth accepted a drink she really didn't want and continued watching bleakly as Sunny twined herself around Daniel. After a moment, she decided she really couldn't stand it and rose to her feet.

'Watch out!'

'Oops!'

'Nick!'

'Too late!'

There was a confused flurry as the photographer stepped backwards, Beth stepped forward and port went flying everywhere. Sunny gave a rueful gasp of laughter.

'Poor Beth! Your dress is ruined. Listen, honey, go look in the closet in the green bedroom and find something to wear. I've got heaps of clothes there.'

Fuming, Beth made her escape. She felt humiliated and ill used as she gained the sanctuary of the bedroom and slammed the door. Was Lane Galloway right? Was this just showbiz or was Daniel calmly flaunting his relationship with another woman at her?

Angrily she pulled open the wardrobe door in search of some clothes and stopped dead. There were clothes there in plenty, rows and rows of them belonging to Sunny. But it wasn't those that caught Beth's eyes, it was the dinner suit Daniel had worn on the night of the fashion show at Cadogan Hall. And next to it, hanging in a neat row, were half a dozen other masculine outfits, which she had no doubt belonged to him too. For a moment Beth was too stunned to take in the implications. Then she gave a bitter laugh. If Daniel was sufficiently at home here to leave his clothes hanging next to Sunny's, was it really likely that they spent their nights together discussing French philosophy and the meaning of life? Of course not! His pursuit of Beth suddenly took on its true significance. A cynical little fling on the side. Well, damn him! Beth wasn't staying around to amuse him any longer.

Scarcely caring what she did, Beth chose an assortment of women's clothes from the hangers. A shirt, jeans, a sweater. None of them fitted properly but it didn't matter because she had no intention of going back and rejoining the party. When she was dressed she slipped out to the kitchen and found Benson alone there doing the dishes. In a few halting words she told him that she had a headache and asked him to present her apologies. Then before he had time to argue with her, she hurried out of the side door and climbed into her car. It took her over three hours to drive back to Buellton and she was in a rage the entire way.

Although it was midsummer the night air was quite chilly when Beth arrived home at the cottage. She paused for a moment looking up at the dark blue sky already studded with stars. A faint breeze stirred in the deodar trees, bringing a fragrance of pine to her nostrils. Somewhere across the valley a dog barked and then was silent. Beth stretched wearily and unlocked the front door. It was cold inside the cottage and she decided that a fire would be cheering. Switching on the light, she went out to the stack of pine logs which Daniel had left handy by the kitchen door. After a few minutes of fussing with kindling and newspaper the pine logs crackled up and filled the living-room with a cheerful glow.

Then, more to avoid the pain of thinking than for any other reason, she brewed herself some peppermint tea with honey. When the fire had settled down to a cosy red glow, she snapped off the light and sat in the big armchair looking into the flames. It would have been a wonderful way to spend an evening if only Daniel had been here with her. But that thought brought back the painful aching realisation that Daniel was with Sunny Martino.

Beth wondered miserably whether there was any way she could stop working for him, but a bargain was a bargain. She had made a commitment and it wasn't only Daniel who depended on her to carry it through. Other women's jobs and livelihoods were tied up with her ability to make the business a success. She had to keep going. All the same, it would be sheer torture to go on living so close to Daniel and to know that he would never give her the love and commitment she craved. Oh, he would have an affair with her readily enough, but that wasn't what she wanted. If only she could cast aside her scruples, Daniel would probably be here sharing her bed tonight. But a faint vestige of sanity made her realise that the pain she was suffering now would be nothing to the pain that would cause her. Well, there was no point brooding over it; it would be much smarter to go to bed alone. Setting down her empty cup, she plodded across towards the stairs that led to her attic bedroom but just as she reached them there was an assertive knock on the front door. Beth froze in her tracks.

'Daniel,' she whispered under her breath.

It was hardly likely to be Jenny or Eric Kronborg, and nobody else would come visiting at this hour of the night. Had he followed her all the way from Los Angeles? And

why? Her heart lurched wildly and she found herself
drawn to the door as if by magnetism. But when she
flung it open, a shock was in store for her.

'You!' she said in dismay.

CHAPTER TEN

IT WASN'T Daniel, it was Warren. He tossed back his silky brown fringe of hair and gave her a leering smile that was obviously meant to be the last word in sensuality.

'Hello, Beth,' he said huskily.

Beth stepped back a pace. 'What are you doing here?' she asked in dismay.

Warren smiled. 'Come on, Beth,' he said in caressing tones. 'That's not very friendly. Anyway you know damn well what I'm doing here. I came because I simply couldn't stay away.'

'Don't be silly,' said Beth sharply.

'Aren't you going to invite me in?' asked Warren.

And without even waiting for an answer he stepped inside and shut the front door, leaning against it. Something about the look on his face made Beth feel deeply uneasy. There was a gloating look of anticipation in his eyes and around the corners of his mouth.

'Please go,' she said in a taut, nervous voice. 'I've already told you, it's over between us.'

Warren took a swaggering step forward.

'You don't expect me to believe that, do you?' he asked. 'We've had our little tiffs in the past, but they've always blown over. I couldn't leave you forever, Beth. I love you too much.'

Beth felt a cold chill settle in the pit of her stomach. Once this declaration would have touched her, but now it only filled her with despair. As he took another two steps towards her she retreated hastily behind the coffee-table.

'You're wasting your time, Warren!' she exclaimed.

'I get it,' said Warren. 'You're still angry about that girl I went to bed with in Los Angeles. But that didn't mean a damn thing, Beth. It's you I'm in love with, not her, and I'm going to prove it to you.'

His eyes in the firelight had a strange glint and too late Beth regretted that she had not switched on the overhead light, but now there was no way she could reach it without passing Warren. And Warren no longer seemed like the petulant boy she had once known. There was a new aura about him that was not only vicious but rather frightening. He took another step towards her, stumbled, and regained his balance, lurching slightly.

'You've been drinking,' said Beth in disgust.

'Well what if I have?' demanded Warren belligerently. 'You're enough to drive me to it, aren't you? All these years you've pretended you loved me but now when we hit the big time you just want to abandon me. It's not fair, Beth, and I won't stand for it. Don't you love me any more?'

He was so close now that Beth could smell the whisky on his breath. She flinched and shook her head.

'I don't think I ever did, Warren,' she said soberly.

'Bitch!' shouted Warren. 'I know what's going on. You're having an affair with that Pryor chap, aren't you?'

'No,' Beth choked.

'Liar!' cried Warren. He grabbed her by the shoulders. 'What's he like in bed?'

Beth tore herself free.

'I have no idea!' she cried acidly. 'And I think you'd better go, Warren.'

'I'm not going till I've had what I came for!' shouted Warren. 'You do it for him, don't you, so why not for me?'

Beth backed away again but found that there was no further room to retreat. Her legs hit the couch and with a muffled gasp she collapsed on to it. A moment later Warren was on top of her, scrabbling at her clothes.

'Let me go,' she shouted, twisting desperately. 'This is ridiculous, Warren. You're drunk! You'll regret it in the morning.'

'The only thing I'll regret is if I don't have you,' insisted Warren. 'I love you, Beth, and I know you love me. You want this just as much as I do.'

'I don't!' cried Beth.

Dragging one hand free, she slapped his face. But Warren snatched her wrist in a cruel grip and stared down at her. For the first time she felt real terror. Then suddenly he lunged forward and ripped open her blouse, exposing the lacy wisps of her bra and her rapidly heaving breasts. Beth tried to struggle free but found herself pinned relentlessly down. She screamed and went on screaming.

'Don't be a fool,' urged Warren, fumbling clumsily at the buckle on his belt. 'I'll marry you if you want me to.'

'I wouldn't marry you if you were the last man alive,' panted Beth, still writhing fiercely in his hold.

His mouth ground down on hers, warm and wet and insistent, making her bite her tongue. She jerked her head to one side and let out an eerie wail of terror.

'Let me go! Let me go!' she cried.

At that moment there was a splintering crash as a door flung open and swift footsteps came racing across the room. Warren was snatched off her body and slammed into one of the walls. He tried to rise groggily to his feet and then collapsed on the floor. Wide-eyed with terror, Beth found herself being hauled to her feet and scrutinised fiercely by Daniel.

'Are you all right?' he demanded. 'He didn't hurt you?'

She gave a dazed sob and shook her head.

'No, I'm all right,' she said.

Daniel swung round and turned his attention to Warren again. Seizing him by the lapels of his shirt, he hauled him to his feet.

'Get out!' he said in a low, deadly voice. 'And thank your lucky stars that we don't prosecute you for this.'

But Warren was still defiant. Lurching slightly, he grabbed at a chair for support and stared at Daniel with an expression of blazing hatred.

'You bastard!' he said. 'You've turned her against me, haven't you? But it's not fair! I did most of the designs in that collection and I'm entitled to the profits. I'll sue you both for this, you just watch me.'

Daniel stared at him with contempt.

'You've been paid and paid generously for anything you did,' he snarled. 'And let me tell you this, buddy. If you ever come near Beth again, you'll really get what's coming to you. But you won't like it, I promise you. Now get out.'

Warren stood swaying thoughtfully for a moment, as if trying to size up whether Daniel's threat was genuine. Evidently he decided it was, for he shrugged suddenly.

'Have it your own way,' he said indistinctly. 'Just gimme my car keys.'

He gestured to a spot on the couch where his keys had fallen from his pocket during his struggle with Beth. Daniel snatched them up.

'No,' he said crisply. 'You're in no condition to drive. You can pick them up from the office tomorrow.'

'But it's four miles to Buellton!' protested Warren.

'Then you'd better start walking right away!' retorted Daniel.

In a series of swift movements he hauled open the front door, swung Warren around and booted him out on to the veranda. Then he slammed the door behind him and tossed the keys into a corner of the room.

'What the hell was he doing here?' he demanded.

Beth gave a half hysterical gulp of laughter. 'Asking me to marry him,' she said, and burst into tears.

Daniel came across and joined her on the sofa. Putting his arms around her, he rocked her gently against him until her shudders subsided.

'I could have killed him,' he snarled. 'I almost did. Are you sure you're all right?'

She swallowed hard, blew her nose and nodded. Her fingers rose unconsciously to a sore place on her chest. She tried to speak and failed. It was hard to believe that the ordeal was over. Daniel took her hand gently in his.

'There's a scratch there,' he said. 'Do you want me to bathe it for you?'

She looked down and realised that Warren's wrist-watch must have grazed her skin. It was nothing serious, but it brought home to her what might have happened. She shuddered again, but shook her head.

'No,' she said huskily. 'I'll be all right now.'

'Are you sure? Isn't there anything I can do for you?'

'Just hold me,' she begged.

His arms tightened protectively around her and he drew her against him. She could hear the rapid, uneven beating of his heart, feel the crisp cotton of his shirt against her cheeks, smell the fragrance of wood-smoke. Bit by bit she began to feel calm again and her breathing steadied. It was almost a pleasure to sit there watching the orange flames flare up the chimney, hearing the hiss

and crackle of the logs and feeling Daniel's arms so safely
about her. I love him, she thought despairingly. Whatever
he's doing with Sunny, I still can't stop loving him. But
it's madness to stay here like this with his arms around
me. She tried to pull away, but he held her gently
imprisoned.

'Why did you run off like that tonight?' he demanded.

In the red glow of the firelight his dark eyes glinted
down at her with a strange expression. Too flustered for
pretence, Beth blurted out the truth.

'Because I couldn't bear to see Sunny Martino all over
you.'

Daniel groaned.

'Beth,' he said, seizing her shoulders and staring at
her intently. 'There is nothing between Sunny and me
which should cause you a moment's pain or unhap-
piness. I swear it.'

He saw the indecision in her face and slowly released
her. Beth gazed back at him, agonisingly conscious of
the way her heart was hammering frantically under his
touch, of the way her mouth felt dry and her breath was
coming in shallow gulps—conscious above all of the
insane urge to cast herself back into his arms. Wordlessly she gazed at him and the silence lengthened. She
heard a clock ticking in the kitchen, saw a log shift and
fall glowing into the embers, smelled the arousing masculine tang of Daniel's body crouched close to her, and
still they both remained motionless. A kind of excitement as potent as a thunderstorm seemed to be
brewing ominously between them, but she felt powerless
to resist it. Sensations she had never dreamed of were
uncoiling deep inside her, sending a fierce pulsating
warmth into every corner of her body. All she could do
was gaze at him, trying to ignore the aching hunger he
woke within her. A muscle twitched sharply in Daniel's

temple and she heard him take a sharp, uneven breath. In that moment she knew without words that he wanted her every bit as badly as she wanted him. Moistening her lips, she tried to speak and failed.

He made as if to rise. 'I'll go, then.'

Beth caught his arm. 'No, don't!' she breathed.

'Sweetheart,' warned Daniel. 'If I don't go now, you know what's going to happen.'

A tremor passed through Beth's body. Yes, she knew. Knew, and gloried in the knowledge. The old warnings clamoured faintly in her head. You might get hurt. He doesn't love you. Men can't be trusted. But they no longer had any power. All she cared about now was that she loved Daniel, and in a moment's blinding insight she knew she would take any risk on earth to be with him.

'It's all right,' she said. 'I want it to happen.'

'Are you sure?' demanded Daniel in a tormented voice.

Her only response was to lean forward into his arms. With a smothered groan he crushed her against him and pressed urgent, devouring kisses on her throat and hair. Deliberately turning her head, she brought her mouth around to his. For an instant she thought he would refuse her even then. But when her trembling, questing lips met his, madness seized them both. Threading his hand savagely through her tumbled hair, Daniel kissed her with an urgency and passion that left her breathless. The room seemed to spiral around her in a dizzying whirl as he bore her ruthlessly down to the floor. She felt the warm tickle of the sheepskin rug under her shoulders, the heat of the fire dancing on her left side and the coolness and darkness to the right of her. But nothing mattered except Daniel's hard, masculine warmth crushing her so satisfyingly into the floor, the scrape of his rough chin against her softness, the frantic thudding of his heart and the way he looked at her. Oh, heavens, how he looked at her! Every plane and angle in his rugged face seemed taut with longing and his eyes flared with an unmistakable savage passion as he kissed her again and again in the firelight. Then suddenly he hauled himself up, so that he was kneeling astride her and gazing fiercely down at her.

'Are you sure you want this?' he demanded hoarsely.

Thrills of excitement pulsed through her entire body and a delicious, melting weakness seemed to overtake her. Reaching up her hand, she caressed his stubbly cheek. I love you, she thought fervently. Oh, Daniel, I love you. But she didn't say it. Instead she simply nodded.

'Yes,' she whispered.

With a sharp intake of breath he was on his feet and hauling off his clothes, flinging them heaven knew where. For a moment he stood there in nothing but his briefs, the fireglow highlighting every muscle and sinew of his magnificent body. He was superbly built, with the powerful shoulders, narrow waist and tapering hips of an athlete. Beth swallowed convulsively when she saw how the firelight turned his skin to bronze, gilding the dark hair on his chest and belly and showing unmistakably the evidence of his arousal. Then slowly, insinuatingly, he peeled off his briefs and lay down beside her. He said nothing, merely looking down at her with the same hungry impatience in his eyes. Then he kissed her again and she let herself yield to wave after wave of throbbing, insistent eagerness. The spicy masculine scent of his body, the skilful, arousing touch of his hands, the urgent warmth of his kisses were driving her to a level of arousal she had never experienced before. And yet beneath the incredulous rapture she felt an aching sense of longing. If only Daniel loved her this would be pure ecstasy, but without love it came dangerously close to torment. Then suddenly his deft fingers stripped away her blouse and the flimsy remnants of her bra and she forgot everything in a blaze of passion that swept over like a forest fire.

Daniel's lips moved over her breasts, warm and teasing and totally shameless. A tingling thrill of pleasure shot through her, making her gasp, and suddenly she was moving in rhythm with him, pressing herself against him, sighing and writhing and offering herself to him. Only when she was ready, maddeningly tormentingly ready, did he go further. She heard his low groan of frustration and her eyelids fluttered open as his hands seized the zip on her jeans. For a moment their eyes met. She could feel her breath coming in rapid, shallow gasps. And she could see the question in his eyes.

'Yes!' she breathed hoarsely.

He was no longer gentle; her remaining clothes were torn free and flung away in a frenzied passion and he rolled wildly with her, pressing her against him so that she ached and burned and shuddered with need, but there was no longer any need for gentleness; both of them were so inflamed with longing that, when at last he entered her, she welcomed him with a cry of gladness. And when they moved together she soared over some invisible edge and turned her face into his neck, gasping his name. He caught her against him, holding her as if he would never let her go and, when he too reached his climax, he seized her hand and kissed it fiercely. Collapsing on top of her, he buried his face in her neck with a long shuddering sigh.

'Oh, Beth,' he groaned.

Her lips twisted in a whimsical smile. Lying there in the firelight, an exalted sense of joy swept through her. Oh, he hadn't told her in so many words that he loved her, but for the first time she felt certain that it was true.

What else could this ecstatic union mean? Turning her
head she kissed him warmly on the cheek.

'Oh, Daniel,' she whispered.

Beth woke slowly the following morning with a drowsy
feeling of contentment. For a moment she lay quietly,
watching the sunlight on the white wall casting filigree
patterns through the lace curtains. Then memory came
rushing back and she rolled hastily over to find Daniel
lying beside her. He was breathing deeply and his face,
relaxed in sleep, looked different from his waking self.
Some of the brooding harshness had vanished and the
tautness around his mouth was softened. He lay on his
side with one arm flung out towards her as if reaching
for her.

Beth propped her chin on her hand and gazed down
at him, smiling wistfully. There was a special kind of
intimacy involved in watching him as he slept and seeing
the way the dark blue and white quilt rose and fell with
his breathing. Holding her breath, she reached out and
stroked the coarse dark hairs on his forearm exper-
imentally. His arm twitched and he made a faint gesture
as if he were dashing away a fly. Suppressing a bubble
of laughter, Beth leaned forward and dropped a butterfly kiss on his cheek. This time he stirred and reached
for her, but still did not wake properly. Beth reached
over the edge of the bed, snatched up a couple of lacy
pillows and thrust them behind her head. Then she leaned
back and resumed the blissful pursuit of watching Daniel.
She had been half aware of him sleeping beside her all
through the night, of his warmth and hardness and length
in the bed, of the deep, regular sound of his breathing,
of the drowsy caress of his hands whenever she strayed
too close to him. But that was nothing to the happiness

she felt now, sitting here wide awake and glorying in his presence.

Memories came hurtling back to her of the previous night. First the jumbled nightmare of Warren's presence, but that was soon banished by a kaleidoscope of passionate, loving sensations. A feeling that was close to reverence took hold of her as she remembered how Daniel had taken her in the firelight. I love him, she thought. And knew that the bond forged between them would last until the day she died. She took in a deep, shuddering breath, wanting to record every detail of the sensations she felt so that this moment would last forever in her mind. She was acutely conscious of the lavender scent of the sheets mingled with the aroma of spicy cologne and a raw tang of masculinity that emanated from Daniel's body. Impulsively she leaned forward and kissed him again. This time one eyebrow rose and a dark eye regarded her sleepily. A faint smile curved the edges of his mouth and then, as suddenly as if a gate had slammed shut, a complete change came over him. He swore softly under his breath and hauled himself up against the bedhead.

'What's wrong?' asked Beth in dismay.

'Everything,' he growled.

Her clenched fist flew up to her mouth and she bit on her knuckles, feeling the pain.

'What do you mean?' she stammered. 'You don't regret what happened, do you?'

He gave a mirthless sneer of laughter and ran his fingers through his dark wavy hair. In spite of her misgivings Beth noticed how the movement sent a ripple through the muscles of his arm and she felt a renewed flicker of desire. But his next words sent a fresh jolt of dismay through her.

'Regret it?' he growled. 'Of course I regret it.'

She cast him a stricken look. He looked back at her, his eyes smouldering with anger or perhaps something else. Then suddenly his face softened and reaching for her, he seized her hair and framed it in twin bunches on either side of her face.

'Don't look like that,' he ordered hoarsely. 'I didn't mean it that way.'

'Then how did you mean it?' she demanded with an edge in her voice. 'Wasn't I exciting enough for you?'

He gave an impatient snarl and released her.

'Exciting?' he retorted. 'You were too damned exciting for my sanity. That's the whole trouble!'

'What do you mean?' asked Beth in alarm.

Daniel leaned back against the polished cedar bedhead and interlaced his strong fingers, offering no reply.

Beth's lips quivered angrily.

'If you don't want me, I wish you'd just come right out and say so!' she exclaimed.

'Want you?' he grated. 'I want you. That's not the problem.'

'Then what is the problem?' demanded Beth.

Daniel's face took on an intense serious look. He caught her by the arms and stared at her with blazing dark eyes.

'This is the problem,' he said through clenched teeth. 'If we continue with this, it may not mean the same thing to both of us.'

Beth felt as sick as if he had suddenly punched her in the stomach. Now I understand, she thought bleakly. He's warning me that he doesn't want to take this relationship seriously, that it won't last forever. For a few seconds she stared at him in anguish and when the words came her voice sounded dry and brittle.

'I don't expect it to be the great love-affair of the century, Daniel,' she said lightly. 'But you told me once

I should take risks and trust my instincts more. Well, I know what my instincts are telling me. I *want* you, Daniel.'

She wanted to say 'love', but the word stuck in her throat. Daniel gave her a bleak, hostile stare.

'That's *all* you want from me?' he asked.

Beth gave him a tormented look. No, it isn't, she wanted to cry. I want more, much more than that. I want you to love me and marry me and give me children and stay with me for the rest of my life. But what a fool she would seem if she said these things aloud!

'Yes, it is,' she said unsteadily. 'That's all I want.'

And reaching forward she touched his cheek and let her hand trail delicately down until it met the rough mat of hair on his chest. Teasingly she let her fingers circle his nipple until she felt the sensitive flesh harden. Then her hand continued down over the hard muscles of his belly, making them clench. Daniel caught his breath and seized her wrist.

'All right,' he said stormily. 'If that's what you want, that's what you'll get.'

His swift movement took her by surprise and a moment later she found herself pinioned against the pillows. His mouth came down on hers in a warm bruising kiss that sent thrills of excitement coursing through her body. Then he drew back and looked into her eyes.

'But there are to be no pressures, do you understand? No high-flown talk about love or permanence. Let's just get to know each other and see how we go. Agreed?'

'Agreed,' whispered Beth.

CHAPTER ELEVEN

THE weeks that followed were a bittersweet time for Beth. In some ways she had never been busier or happier. She shared with Daniel many of the headaches and excitements of her expanding business. And there were leisure activities as well. Trail rides up in the hills, kayaking on the off-shore islands near Santa Barbara, picnics and swimming on the white sandy beaches that fringed the coast, and pleasant outdoor lunches in the quaint Danish village of Solvang. Not to mention nights of shared passion when she felt as if the earth had tilted on its axis and would never be the same again.

But, like a discordant counterpoint to all this happiness, Beth felt a growing sense of misgiving. However much shared passion and work and laughter their lives might have, she had the frustrating sense that she was not growing any closer to Daniel. In fact most of the time she felt as if he was deliberately pushing her away. Although they made love with urgent frequency, he never again spent an entire night in her cottage, always preferring to go home to his own house. He never talked to her about his feelings towards her. And, what was worst of all, he seemed to be spending more time than ever in the company of Sunny Martino.

Not that Beth thought Daniel was actually sleeping with the actress. He couldn't be cynical or callous enough for that, surely? And yet she found her beliefs on this subject swinging wildly between two totally opposite poles. In the moments late at night when Daniel gasped her name and crushed her against him in the lamplight,

Beth knew she was totally and utterly foolish even to imagine such a thing. Yet in daylight the suspicion refused to die. When Daniel went away for days at a time to Los Angeles or on the two occasions when he brought Sunny back to spend a weekend at the farm, Beth found herself a prey to a jealousy that both shocked and appalled her.

And the trouble was that she didn't know what to do about it. She thought of tackling Daniel and demanding the truth, but it was an ordeal she didn't want to face. Perhaps because the pain of learning that he was still Sunny's lover would be more than she could bear. Or even because she still foolishly cherished the hope that one day Daniel would tell her he loved her and ask her to marry him. The mere notion brought a dry, mirthless laugh to her lips. What a fool she was!

Of course, she could have asked Sunny point-blank what was happening but pride made her shrink from that. It would be far too embarrassing. There were even moments when she felt a certain painful sympathy with the actress. If Sunny loved Daniel, the whole situation must be just as agonising for her as it was for Beth. Yet, on the few occasions when Beth saw her, she didn't seem in much agony. She was pert, lively and full of studio gossip. And her flirtatious manner towards Daniel seemed as much a part of her as her magnificent bosom or her scarlet fingernails. Even if she is involved with him, thought Beth miserably, I don't believe it matters to her the way it does to me. I should do something, she told herself despairingly. I shouldn't just drift like this. In a moment of grim insight she knew she had let herself be caught in exactly the trap that she dreaded. A relationship without trust, without hope, without a future. And her joy in Daniel's company began to give way to a smouldering resentment. I am not going to put up with this forever, she vowed. One of these days he'll go too far and he'll get the shock of his life.

By the end of July, Beth's winter collection of clothes was completed and ready for the new season's fashion shows in Los Angeles. A month of hard labour had gone into the preparations and, when Daniel suggested a weekend's sailing in Santa Barbara, Beth was only too happy to agree. Out in the lazy blue tranquillity of the Pacific Ocean with nothing but the hot sun overhead, the creak of the rigging, the lazy slap of the dark blue sea against the hull, it was easy to believe that everything would come right between her and Daniel. Yet Sunny managed to ruin even this simple pleasure. As they were heading back for home, there was a call on the radiophone.

'Who is it?' asked Beth sleepily without much interest. She was lying on the deck, creaming sunscreen over her shoulders for a carefully timed tan.

'Benson,' replied Daniel, switching off the phone. 'He said Sunny called about half an hour ago and says she has been on location up near San Francisco. She's driving through to Los Angeles and wants to stop for supper with us around seven. Is that OK with you?'

'Yes, of course,' said Beth rather frostily.

The request brought home the difficulty of her situation. Even if she were married to Daniel, there might well be times when he would entertain people whom she didn't particularly want, but not his mistress, surely? The thought sent a familiar barb of pain through her. Was Sunny his mistress? Beth stared down at him with a troubled expression, wishing she could read his mind, wishing he would tell her what was going on.

'What's wrong?' he asked sharply, intercepting her look.

'Nothing,' she said huskily, managing a small unconvincing smile.

He stretched out his hand to her.

'Come here,' he ordered gruffly.

She slid down into the cockpit on the padded seat beside him. His right hand still held the tiller, but his left arm came round her and drew her firmly against him. So close that she could feel the warmth of his tanned thigh against hers and feel the rise and fall of his chest as he breathed.

'Are you happy with me?' he demanded harshly.

She nodded silently, letting her long fingers trail along the inside of his leg. She wondered bitterly why it was so easy to touch him intimately yet so hard to speak to him of her feelings.

'No regrets?' he demanded.

She sighed.

'No regrets,' she said bleakly.

It was after six o'clock when they reached Daniel's house in the hills and delectable smells of fried chicken were issuing from the kitchen. Benson came out into the living-room to greet them.

'I wonder if I could persuade you to join me in the kitchen, Miss Saxon,' he suggested with a smile. 'I thought I might try that new potato salad recipe you were telling me about.'

'Yes, of course,' said Beth, feeling rather flattered.

In the couple of months since she had first met Daniel, she had struck up quite a friendship with the reserved British butler. She suspected he was probably rather like herself, someone with strong feelings who found it very hard to express them. When she had showered and changed she made her way to the kitchen, with the comfortable feeling of joining a friend. She found it was quite soothing to fry chips of bacon and chop up parsley while Benson chatted about his years in the British navy. Fortunately he already had some cold boiled potatoes ready in the refrigerator, so all she had to do was add the chopped hard-boiled eggs, the bacon, parsley and mayonnaise and a plentiful grinding of black pepper.

'There,' she said with satisfaction.

'May I taste it?' asked Benson, scooping some on a saucer with a fork. 'Yes, that's excellent. You know it reminds me of a lunch I had with my late wife Barbara ten years ago in Torquay. Funny how the taste of food can take you back, isn't it? I can see our cottage now, with the sea below us and the red geraniums on the terrace.'

'That sounds lovely,' said Beth sincerely. 'Did you miss it when you moved to the United States?'

'Oh, yes,' agreed Benson. 'But I felt a complete break was best after Barbara's death. My sons were both grown-up and didn't need me and Mr Pryor offered me a very tempting salary to come here and work for him. Very tempting indeed. And I always told him I would stay with him until he got married then I'd retire back to Torquay. Well, it looks as though I won't have long to wait now, doesn't it?'

'What?' echoed Beth aghast. 'What do you mean?'

Benson cleared his throat and looked embarrassed.

'Oh, well, I'll say no more,' he apologised. 'Perhaps I've already said too much.'

Beth was still looking at him in consternation when the front doorbell suddenly rang.

'Would you mind going, madam?' asked Benson. 'I've got my hands covered in flour and I doubt if Mr Pryor will hear it, shut away with that computer going.'

'Not at all,' agreed Beth.

She hurried out of the kitchen into the hall with her thoughts whirling. Was Benson implying that Daniel was about to get married? Well, if so, it certainly couldn't be Beth that he had in mind, for he had never mentioned anything of the kind to her. And that only left one possibility. Sunny Martino! Beth reached the doorway of the living-room and stood frozen in her tracks. Obviously Daniel had heard the doorbell, for he was striding towards the front door with an eager smile on his face. As he opened the door, Sunny burst in and flung herself on his neck. Daniel swung her around in a circle and then set her on her feet again, whistling a snatch of that poignant little tune that Beth had first heard on the day of their trail ride.

'Well, how are you doing, Sunny?' he asked.

Sunny gave a low, sensual ripple of laughter and then stood on tiptoe lifting her lips to his.

'Oh, it's torture to go on seeing you like this, my darling,' she trilled. 'But soon the waiting will be over. The moment my divorce comes through we can be married at last. I can't wait for the day!'

Beth didn't wait to hear any more. An incredulous feeling of horror filled her as she backed away through the living-room and she was conscious of only one thing. The need to get as far away as possible.

Incredibly Benson was still in the kitchen frying chicken when she returned. She felt as if years must have passed and yet it couldn't have been more than five minutes. With a dazed expression she looked about her, half expecting to see something like the devastation of the big San Francisco earthquake. Something to match the way she felt inside. But the kitchen looked just as always.

'I'm leaving now!' she blurted out.

Benson looked shocked. Or at least, if Benson had ever shown his feelings, he would have looked shocked.

Both grey eyebrows rose by almost a millimetre and his lips pursed.

'Indeed, madam? You're not hungry?'

'No. No! Benson, I have to... I have to go. I've forgotten something in... Los Angeles. The wedding-dress for the auction tomorrow. It needs more seed-pearls sewn on the hem.'

Benson sniffed.

'Will there be any message for Mr Pryor, madam?'

Beth's eyes shot blue fire. 'Yes! Tell him... tell him... oh, what's the use?'

Hastily biting her knuckle, she ran out of the room. There was no pursuit. Benson was like the three wise monkeys. 'See no evil, hear no evil, speak no evil' was his motto, and he didn't believe in interfering. And of course Daniel was too busy dancing attention on Sunny Martino out on the patio to care what Beth was doing. She saw their surprised faces as her car roared down the drive and felt a momentary surge of satisfaction. But it soon gave way to despair.

As she drove down the coast road every mile was filled with memories of Daniel. She could not breathe the salt air or see the dark mechanical shapes of the oil rigs against the red blaze of the setting sun without thinking of him. Was it really only a couple of months since they had driven down this road together for her first fashion show in Los Angeles? She thought of all that had happened since then and an ache like a physical pain spread through her body. Try as she might, she could not stem the flood of memories. Daniel fishing her out of the Santa Barbara harbour in her wedding-dress, cajoling and bullying her into the frenzied task of replacing her lost fashion collection. Daniel in the candlelight at Emilio's, his eyes glittering as he told her how much he wanted her. Daniel on the trail ride, looking totally at home in the saddle with blue sky and sun-bleached hills all around him. Daniel's kindness and patience as he started the young filly, his rage as he hurled Warren into the night, his passion as he made love to Beth in the red glare of the firelight. And now his betrayal.

'I can't bear it!' she said aloud. 'I can't bear it.'

Although it was Sunday, the traffic in the centre of the city seemed almost as gridlocked as on a weekday and it was almost three hours before she reached Daniel's apartment block. When she did, she sat outside, hesitating as she looked at the familiar palm trees and the pale blue plumbago spilling over the side wall. The first place Daniel would look for her was her cottage in the Santa Ynez Valley, but after that he would certainly come here. And he wouldn't be in a good mood. Beth winced, dreading the inevitable confrontation. Sooner or later she would have to talk to him, but tonight she simply couldn't face it. That left only one place she could go. The shop on Rodeo Drive.

It was close to midnight when she arrived there and the couch in the tearoom was just as uncomfortable as it looked. She lay awake for a long time, staring into the darkness, her throat aching with unshed tears. About two a.m. she drifted into a light doze, but was startled into consciousness by the clamour of the telephone. She jumped up and ran to it, but froze as her fingers touched the receiver. Daniel. It could only be Daniel. And she didn't want to speak to him. Not now. Not ever. She let it shrill on and on, feeling as if every nerve in her body was in torment, until at last it stopped.

Yet she could not postpone the ordeal forever. The next morning she was at Cadogan Hall bright and early, dressed in a stylish blue honeycomb-knit dress with enough make-up to cover her pallor. As she helped the models dress and listened to the murmur of the growing

audience in the hall, she half feared and half hoped that
Daniel would come and find her. But he didn't. The
thunderous applause at the end of her show assured her
that her designs had been a success, but she scarcely
cared. Her stomach was churning nervously and only
guilt and a sense of duty brought her out into the
audience to watch the wedding-dress being auctioned for
charity.

She saw him then and her heart missed a beat at the
sight. He was wearing a pale grey suit with a blue shirt
and striped tie and one glance was enough to tell her
that he was seething. He sat forward in his place with
his elbows resting tautly on his knees and his chin jutting
forward. When his gaze met Beth's he glanced instantly
away and said something to the woman beside him.
Beth's spirits sank as she realised it was Sunny Martino.

Even the auction of the wedding-dress wasn't enough
to take her mind off Daniel, although the bidding seemed
to be climbing to astronomical heights. It was a dream
of a dress in white organza with puffed sleeves, a lace
overskirt, a dramatic train and a bodice and hem em-
broidered with tiny seed-pearls. Beth's eyes widened as
the final bid was announced and a bald, middle-aged
man came forward to claim his trophy. Forty thousand
dollars! It was unbelievable. Then her gaze slewed back
to Daniel.

He was coming towards her with a grim smile playing
around the corners of his mouth and an unholy light
blazing in his eyes. As he reached her he gave her a curt
nod.

'Hello, Beth. May I take you upstairs to lunch?'

'Well, I——'

'Good.'

His fingers closed around her arm like a vice. This
time there was no insistence on sending her off to fend

for herself. Throughout the next hour he stayed beside her while buyers came to her with orders, photographers clustered to take her photo and the gossip columnists surged around interviewing her. Not that anyone would have been tempted to suppose he was in love with her. His expression was frankly murderous.

'Right, we're getting out of here,' he announced at precisely two o'clock.

'I don't want to leave yet!' protested Beth.

'Sweetheart,' growled Daniel in a voice that sent thrills of panic chasing down her spine, 'we have business to discuss and, unless you want to discuss it here, we're leaving now.'

The drive home passed in ominous silence. Daniel ignored her tentative attempts at conversation, clearly determined to have the showdown on his own ground. Only when they were inside his apartment and the door had slammed shut behind them did he speak.

'Well?' he said in a soft, menacing tone as he advanced towards her. 'Running out on me seems to be getting quite a habit of yours. Would you mind telling me why you left me this time?'

Beth felt a flicker of alarm at the controlled rage in every line of his powerful body. Then an answering spark of anger flared up inside her, like a cinder whipped by a sudden wind.

'No, I wouldn't mind at all!' she retorted, tossing her head. 'I left because I'm not prepared to share you with Sunny Martino. Or anyone else.'

'Share me with Sunny Martino? What the hell are you talking about?'

His shock and outrage were so blatant that Beth paused for a moment. Could she possibly have made a mistake? Then she remembered her conversation with

Benson and the words she had overheard between Sunny and Daniel and her anger flared up again.

'You know perfectly well what I'm talking about!' she exclaimed. 'Benson dropped me a pretty broad hint that you were planning on getting married and I overheard that stuff that Sunny told you at the door last night about how it was torture to go on seeing you and how she was going to marry you the minute her divorce came through... What are you laughing at?'

For to her astonishment Daniel's stern expression had suddenly broken up. He stood staring at her for a moment, with twitching lips and gleaming eyes and then it was all too much for him, and he laughed until the tears came to his eyes. Beth watched coldly, wondering if he had lost his senses. At last he straightened up and shook his head, but even then his words made no sense.

'I'll be darned. *Destiny's Favourite*.'

'What are you talking about?' demanded Beth in a hostile voice.

Daniel was still grinning and shaking his head but he managed to compose himself enough to whistle a few bars of a haunting little tune. The poignant melody that Beth had first heard on the trail ride. Then the notes petered out.

'I'm not going to marry Sunny,' he said flatly. 'What you heard from her wasn't a statement of undying passion, it was the opening lines from *Destiny's Favourite*. Hell, that scene must have been played fifty times or more on television. It's a private joke between Sunny and me.'

'Then you're not in love with her?' said Beth uncertainly.

'No.'

Beth bit her lip, feeling humiliated and very, very foolish. The half-hidden grin on Daniel's face didn't help matters much. Angrily she pushed past him into the living-room.

'Well, you can hardly blame me for thinking that you were,' she flared. 'Heaven knows you've done your best to make me believe that ever since I first met you.'

She heard Daniel's footsteps behind her. His voice was suddenly sober.

'That's true,' he admitted, his warm hand descending on her shoulder. 'I wanted you to think that.'

She swung round to face him, anger surging through her.

'Why?' she demanded. 'Just to get a good laugh out of how stupid I was?'

'No,' insisted Daniel. 'Look, at first it was just to throw the reporters off our trail, but after that I kept it up because I wanted to make you jealous.'

'Jealous! Why?'

Daniel winced and seemed to search vainly for words.

'Oh, I can't explain it,' he said impatiently. 'It was all to do with Warren. I thought if you got the idea that Sunny was keen on me you'd realise you wanted me more than him and you'd give him up.'

Beth gave a mirthless laugh.

'You could have saved yourself the trouble,' she said. 'I gave up Warren the morning after the first fashion show. I just couldn't keep on seeing him when I was so attracted to you.'

Daniel let out a long, bewildered sigh and ran his fingers through his hair.

'Well, if you were so attracted to me, why were you always fighting me off?' he demanded.

Beth felt as if she was skating on very thin ice. The memory of Greg flashed back to haunt her, but curiously it no longer seemed to have any power. She shrugged.

'You reminded me of someone,' she said. 'Someone I knew a long time ago.'

But Daniel was shrewd.

'The guy you were involved with before you started seeing Warren?' he demanded.

'I suppose you could say that,' said Beth with an uneasy grimace.

Daniel's eyes were narrowed and hostile.

'Who was he?' he rapped out.

Beth flinched.

'My sister's husband,' she said.

'You had an affair with your sister's husband?' echoed Daniel in horror.

'No!' cried Beth. 'He—he kissed me once. It made me feel terrible. Guilty, ashamed, distrustful of men with that kind of raw animal magnetism, men who had meaningless affairs with women they didn't care about. When I met you, you reminded me of him.'

'Thanks,' said Daniel wryly. 'I appreciate the character analysis. But it may interest you to know that I fell in love with you the first day I met you and my intentions towards you have never been anything but honourable.'

Beth stared at him in shock, unable to believe what she had just heard.

'Why didn't you tell me?' she asked slowly.

Daniel paced angrily around the room, clenching and unclenching his fists.

'Because you were involved with Warren,' he said. 'Or I thought you were. And also because you accused me of manipulating and railroading people. There was enough truth in that accusation to make it hurt. And I sure as hell didn't want to railroad you. I wanted you to be certain of your feelings for me, so I never told you how much I loved you for fear of putting pressure on you. But maybe Sunny was right. She always insisted that I ought to tell you the truth.'

Beth stared at him in shock.

'Sunny insisted?' she demanded. 'You discussed this with Sunny?'

Daniel nodded. 'We're very old friends,' he said.

'Not lovers?' demanded Beth suspiciously.

'No,' insisted Daniel. 'We never have been. I'm very fond of Sunny but that's all there is to it.'

'But you stay overnight with her! You keep your clothes in her closet!'

'In her spare bedroom closet,' retorted Daniel. 'Staying overnight saves me time dodging the traffic. Besides, I like to play pool with Sunny's husband.'

'Sunny's husband?' echoed Beth in astonishment.

Daniel grinned.

'Yes. She married Lane Galloway last year, although that's the best-kept secret in town, so don't let it out.'

'But why doesn't she want anyone to know?' asked Beth, momentarily diverted.

Daniel brushed her question aside impatiently. 'Because they're both heart-throbs of the silver screen,' he said. 'The fans wouldn't like it. But never mind that. It's us I want to talk about, not them. I love you, Beth. More than any woman I've ever known.'

Beth stared at him doubtfully.

'Even the one who turned you down?' she asked. 'The one you told me about on the trail ride?'

'Susan? Hell, yes! She was a fellow law student at Harvard and once I quit law she didn't want to know me. All she was interested in was money and status, not me. But that experience really made its mark on me. I never fell in love again. Until I met you.'

'You really mean to tell me that you've loved me all this time and you've never said a word about it?' she demanded.

Daniel made an impatient movement with his hands.

'I thought you'd guess,' he said. 'From the way I looked at you. The way I touched you. The way I made love to you. Wasn't that enough?'

'It was magical,' Beth admitted huskily. 'But I wanted more than that. I wanted love too. I wanted to know where I stood.'

Daniel reached out his hand and trailed it caressingly down her face and on to her shoulder.

'Come into the bedroom with me,' he said hoarsely. 'I'll show you where you stand.'

Beth stepped back out of reach.

'No,' she said in torment. 'You know, it's kind of ironical, Daniel, but you told me once that I should assert myself and you were damn right. Well, I'm doing it now. I don't just want love, I want everything. Marriage, children, a home. And if I can't have all of that from you, I don't want any more to do with you. Telling someone you love them is easy enough, but how much does it really mean? Not much. Certainly not enough to make me jump into bed with you any more.'

Daniel's eyes met hers full of naked, glittering emotion.

'I'm serious, Beth,' he said. 'Come with me. I promise I won't touch you, if you don't want me to. But there's something you must see.'

Seizing her hand, he led the way across the hall and flung open the bedroom door. Uneasily Beth stepped inside and then caught her breath. A warm, sweet perfume filled the air. Gazing around her, she saw that the entire room was filled with white roses and carnations. Laid out on the centre of the bed was the wedding-dress that had been auctioned at the fashion show, a dream of frothing white lace and organza. She turned with a question in her eyes.

'How did this get here?' she demanded.

'I bought it,' said Daniel.

'But the bald man ...'

'My attorney, acting on my behalf.'

Beth bit her lip and walked over to the bed. With trembling fingers she picked up the dress and held it against her.

'Why?' she breathed.

Daniel's lips twisted into a smile.

'Isn't that obvious? I want you to wear it on our wedding-day. Will you?'

Beth's heart gave a violent lurch and suddenly she was in his arms with the dress crushed between them.

'Yes. Oh, yes,' she exclaimed joyfully.

His lips came down on hers in a long, bruising kiss and the dress fell unnoticed to the floor. Winding her arms around his neck Beth stood on tiptoe and whispered in his ear.

'Daniel,' she said unsteadily. 'Could I change my mind about jumping into bed with you?'

She felt rather than heard his low rumble of laughter.

'Be my guest,' he invited.

An hour later as they lay naked and sated together, Beth raised herself on one elbow and trailed her fingers through the dark mat of hair on Daniel's chest.

'Daniel?' she said curiously.

'Mmm?'

'How did Benson know you were going to get married? Did you have the hide to tell him before you proposed to me?'

Daniel looked shifty.

'Hell, no, honey,' he said in injured tones. 'All I did was ask him what would be the best place to hold a wedding reception. And maybe I did drop him another slight hint.'

'What kind of hint?' asked Beth suspiciously.

'Well, I just said, ''Benson, don't you think Beth will be the most beautiful bride Santa Barbara has ever seen?'' '

Beth gave an incredulous gasp of laughter.

'And what did he say?' she demanded.

Daniel gathered her in his arms and began kissing her all the way down her throat to her breasts, punctuating his words with kisses.

'What...could he say...? He said...yes...of course.'

TASTY FOOD COMPETITION!

How would you like a years supply of Mills & Boon Romances ABSOLUTELY FREE? Well, you can win them! All you have to do is complete the word puzzle below and send it in to us by 30th June 1994. The first 5 correct entries picked out of the bag after that date will win a years supply of Mills & Boon Romances (*four books every month - worth over £90*) What could be easier?

```
H O L L A N D A I S E R
E Y E G G O W H A O H A
R S E E C L A I R U C T
B T K K A E T S I F I A
E E T I S M A L C F U T
U R C M T L H E E L Q O
G S I U T F O N O E D U
N H L S O T O N E F M I
I S R S O M A C W A A L
R I A E E T I R J A E L
E F G L L P T O T V R E
M O U S S E E O D O C P
```

CLAM	HOLLANDAISE	OYSTERS	SPICE
COD	JAM	PRAWN	STEAK
CREAM	LEEK	QUICHE	TART
ECLAIR	LEMON	RATATOUILLE	
EGG	MELON	RICE	
FISH	MERINGUE	RISOTTO	
GARLIC	MOUSSE	SALT	
HERB	MUSSELS	SOUFFLE	

PLEASE TURN OVER FOR DETAILS ON HOW TO ENTER ➡

HOW TO ENTER

All the words listed overleaf, below the word puzzle, are hidden in the grid. You can find them by reading the letters forward, backwards, up or down, or diagonally. When you find a word, circle it or put a line through it, the remaining letters (which you can read from left to right, from the top of the puzzle through to the bottom) will ask a romantic question.

After you have filled in all the words, don't forget to fill in your name and address in the space provided and pop this page in an envelope (you don't need a stamp) and post it today. Hurry – competition ends 30th June 1994.

Mills & Boon Tasty Food Competition,
FREEPOST,
P.O. Box 236,
Croydon,
Surrey. CR9 9EL

Hidden Question _____

_____

Are you a Reader Service Subscriber?   Yes ☐ No ☐

Ms/Mrs/Miss/Mr _____

Address _____

_____

_____ Postcode _____

mps
MAILING
PREFERENCE
SERVICE

COMTF

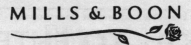

MILLS & BOON

NEW LOOK MILLS & BOON ROMANCES

A few months ago we introduced new look covers on our Romance series and we'd like to hear just how much you like them.

Please spare a few minutes to answer the questions below and we will send you a **FREE** Mills & Boon novel as a thank you. Just send the completed questionnaire back to us today - **NO STAMP NEEDED**.

Don't forget to fill in your name and address, so that we know where to send your **FREE** book!

Please tick the appropriate box to indicate your answers. ✔

1. **For how long have you been a Mills & Boon Romance reader?**

Since the new covers ☐	1 to 2 years ☐	6 to 10 years ☐
Less than 1 year ☐	3 to 5 years ☐	Over 10 years ☐

2. **How frequently do you read Mills & Boon Romances?**

Every Month ☐   Every 2 to 3 Months ☐   Less Often ☐

3. **From where do you usually obtain your Romances?**

Mills & Boon Reader Service ☐   Supermarket ☐

W H Smith/John Menzies/Other Newsagent ☐

Boots/Woolworths/Department Store ☐

Other (please specify:) _____

4. **Please let us know how much you like the new covers:**

Like very much ☐   Don't like very much ☐

Like quite a lot ☐   Don't like at all ☐

5. **What do you like most about the design of the covers?** _____

_____

_____

6. **What do you like least about the design of the covers?** _____

_____

_____

7. **Do you have any additional comments you'd like to make about our new look Romances?** _____

_____

_____

8. **Do you read any other Mills & Boon series? (Please tick each series you read).**

Love on Call (Medical Romances) ☐   Temptation ☐

Legacy of Love (Masquerade) ☐   Duet ☐

Favourites (Best Sellers) ☐   Don't read any others ☐

9. **Are you a Reader Service subscriber?**

Yes ☐   No ☐

If Yes, what is your subscriber number? _____

10. **What is your age group?**

16-24 ☐   25-34 ☐   35-44 ☐   45-54 ☐   55-64 ☐   65+ ☐

THANK YOU FOR YOUR HELP

✉   Please send your completed questionnaire to: ✉

Mills & Boon Reader Service, FREEPOST,
P O Box 236, Croydon, Surrey CR9 9EL

NO STAMP NEEDED

Ms/Mrs/Miss/Mr: _____ NR

Address: _____

_____

_____ Postcode: _____

You may be mailed with offers from other reputable companies as a result of this
application. Please tick box if you would prefer not to receive such offers. ☐
One application per household.

mps MAILING PREFERENCE SERVICE

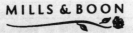

Next Month's Romances

Each month you can choose from a wide variety of romance with Mills & Boon. Below are the new titles to look out for next month, why not ask either Mills & Boon Reader Service or your Newsagent to reserve you a copy of the titles you want to buy – just tick the titles you would like and either post to Reader Service or take it to any Newsagent and ask them to order your books.

Please save me the following titles:	**Please tick**	√
HEART-THROB FOR HIRE	Miranda Lee	
A SECRET REBELLION	Anne Mather	
THE CRUELLEST LIE	Susan Napier	
THE AWAKENED HEART	Betty Neels	
ITALIAN INVADER	Jessica Steele	
A RECKLESS ATTRACTION	Kay Thorpe	
BITTER HONEY	Helen Brooks	
THE POWER OF LOVE	Rosemary Hammond	
MASTER OF DECEIT	Susanne McCarthy	
THE TOUCH OF APHRODITE	Joanna Mansell	
POSSESSED BY LOVE	Natalie Fox	
GOLDEN MISTRESS	Angela Wells	
NOT FOR LOVE	Pamela Hatton	
SHATTERED MIRROR	Kate Walker	
A MOST CONVENIENT MARRIAGE	Suzanne Carey	
TEMPORARY MEASURES	Leigh Michaels	

If you would like to order these books in addition to your regular subscription from Mills & Boon Reader Service please send £1.80 per title to: Mills & Boon Reader Service, Freepost, P.O. Box 236, Croydon, Surrey, CR9 9EL, quote your Subscriber No:.................... (If applicable) and complete the name and address details below. Alternatively, these books are available from many local Newsagents including W.H.Smith, J.Menzies, Martins and other paperback stockists from 11 February 1994.

Name:...

Address:..

....Post Code:..........................

To Retailer: If you would like to stock M&B books please contact your regular book/magazine wholesaler for details.

You may be mailed with offers from other reputable companies as a result of this application. If you would rather not take advantage of these opportunities please tick box ☐